THE
HAUNTED CAR

GOOSEBUMPS®
HALL OF HORRORS

#1 CLAWS!
#2 NIGHT OF THE GIANT EVERYTHING
#3 SPECIAL EDITION: THE FIVE MASKS OF DR. SCREEM
#4 WHY I QUIT ZOMBIE SCHOOL
#5 DON'T SCREAM!
#6 THE BIRTHDAY PARTY OF NO RETURN

GOOSEBUMPS® WANTED:
THE HAUNTED MASK

GOOSEBUMPS®
MOST WANTED

#1 PLANET OF THE LAWN GNOMES
#2 SON OF SLAPPY
#3 HOW I MET MY MONSTER
#4 FRANKENSTEIN'S DOG
#5 DR. MANIAC WILL SEE YOU NOW
#6 CREATURE TEACHER: FINAL EXAM
#7 A NIGHTMARE ON CLOWN STREET

SPECIAL EDITION #1 ZOMBIE HALLOWEEN
SPECIAL EDITION #2 THE 12 SCREAMS OF CHRISTMAS
SPECIAL EDITION #3 TRICK OR TRAP

Goosebumps®

THE HAUNTED CAR

R.L. STINE

SCHOLASTIC INC.

Goosebumps book series created by Parachute Press, Inc.
Copyright © 1999 by Scholastic Inc.

Originally published as *Goosebumps Series 2000 #21: The Haunted Car*

All rights reserved. Published by Scholastic Inc., *Publishers since 1920*. SCHOLASTIC, GOOSEBUMPS, GOOSEBUMPS HORRORLAND, and associated logos are trademarks and/or registered trademarks of Scholastic Inc.

ISBN 978-0-545-82885-7

12 11 10   16 17 18 19/0

Printed in the U.S.A.   40
This edition first printing, May 2015

I have a '57 Chevy Impala in my room. It's two-tone blue with red-and-silver flame detailing on the sides and fins.

And I have a '92 Firebird V-8 with a twin-cam engine and black leather interior. And I have an '83 silver Camaro that I haven't finished putting together.

Yes, they're models. I've filled the bookshelves along my bedroom wall with model cars that I've built.

Dad says he's going to build shelves on the other wall to hold the new ones. But that would cover up my race car posters.

I don't want to do that. I love my car posters. One of them is even signed by Mario Andretti. If you're not into cars, I'd better explain that he's a very famous race car driver. In fact, he's a legend.

My name is Mitchell Moinian. I'm twelve, and I'm kind of a legend, too. That's because I know more about cars than anybody in my school.

1

Sometimes my friends Allan and Steve and I have a contest. We stand on the corner outside my house and see who can be the first to identify the cars that come by.

I win every time. I can identify cars with my eyes closed!

That's because I read stacks and stacks of car magazines. And when I'm not reading about cars or building models of cars, I like to draw cars.

Know what I dream about at night? That's right — I dream that I'm *driving* cars.

Anyway, I guess my story starts on a peaceful Saturday afternoon. It had rained all morning, and a few raindrops, blown by the wind, still tapped against my bedroom window.

I didn't care. I like the sound of rain when I'm inside working on a model. I leaned over my worktable, studying the diagrams for the silver Camaro.

It was pretty complicated. There were a million pieces to this one. I mean, you don't just glue slot A to tab B and call it a Camaro!

I had the chassis built. And I was carefully fitting together fiberglass parts to the body — when my brother, Todd, came bursting into the room, screaming his head off.

"Hey!" I jumped — and cracked a fender. The fiberglass split in my fist.

"You jerk!" I screamed. "Look what you made me do!"

2

Todd didn't even look down at the broken fender. "Hurry! Help me!" he cried. "You've got to come — quick!"

Todd is seven. He's not into cars. I don't know what he's into.

I guess he's into scaring himself. He's been very weird ever since we moved into this creepy old house last year.

We had a perfectly nice house back in Toledo. But Dad got a new job, and we had to move to Forrest Valley. And Mom and Dad bought this huge, old, broken-down heap.

The house leans over a high peak on the top of Hunter Hill. You can see our house from town in Forrest Valley below. Even from so far away, the house looks like a haunted house in a horror movie.

I think they bought this wreck because Dad likes to build and repair things. He watches all those "Fix Up Your Own House" shows on TV and says, "I can do that. I can do that."

Except he really can't.

As Mom says, "When it comes to being handy, he's all thumbs!"

Anyway, Todd has been acting really weird ever since we moved in. He is convinced the house is haunted. He's always seeing ghosts in every room.

He's always screaming and carrying on and freaking himself out. Do you believe it? The poor guy has to sleep with his lights on!

And now he stood trembling in my doorway, motioning frantically with both hands for me to follow him. He's so skinny and blond and pink. I had to laugh. The way he was twitching and shaking, he looked like a frightened bunny rabbit.

"Mitchell — hurry! Please!" he cried. "There's a ghost in my room!"

"Not again," I groaned. I dropped the broken fiberglass fender to the table and glared at my brother. "Todd, your *brain* is haunted. How many times do I have to tell you? There's no ghost in this house!"

"Please —" he pleaded.

"Have you been reading those scary books again?" I asked. "You know you're too young for them."

"No. Really. I'm not making it up this time," he insisted. He turned and gazed down the hall, quivering all over. "It — it's down there."

"Okay, okay," I muttered. I climbed to my feet, shaking my head. "You wrecked my Camaro fender. There'd better be a real ghost this time."

"There is," he murmured. "For real. In my closet. I saw it."

He stepped aside to let me pass. I peered down the long, dark hallway. Gray light washed in from the tiny window at the far end. Dad had started to put up ceiling lights. But he needed someone to help him with the wiring.

In the meantime, the long hall was always dark. And the ancient brown wallpaper on the walls, cracked and peeling, didn't make it any brighter.

The old floorboards creaked under our feet as I led the way to Todd's room.

"A ghost in my closet," Todd whispered. "I'm not making it up."

He stayed behind me, one hand clinging to the back of my T-shirt. I glanced over my shoulder. His bunny face twitched, blue eyes wide with fright.

Todd always was the weird one in the Moinian family. He doesn't even look like us. Mom, Dad, and I are all tall and dark, with brown eyes and brown hair.

I stopped at the doorway and peered into Todd's room. Gloomy gray light washed over the room from the rain-spotted window.

"Do you see it? Do you see it?" Todd eagerly whispered behind me, his fist still clinging to my shirt.

"Of course not —" I started.

But then my eyes moved to Todd's half-open closet door. And I saw the ghostly figure floating inside the closet.

"Whoa," I murmured. A chill of fear rolled down my body.

"What? You see it? What is it?" Todd demanded, his fist jabbing my back.

I squinted into the gray light, struggling to focus, watching the pale, unmoving figure.

It took me a few seconds to realize that I wasn't staring at a ghost. I was staring at Todd's half-full laundry bag.

"You jerk!" I cried. I turned and gave him a hard shove with both hands. "It's your laundry bag!"

He stumbled backward and hit the wall. "Well, who would leave it there?" he demanded. "How was I supposed to know it wasn't a ghost?"

"Because there aren't any ghosts!" I screamed.

"Prove it," he replied. He crossed his bony arms over the front of his *X-Files* T-shirt.

"Prove what?" I snarled. "Prove that there aren't any ghosts?"

"The truth is out there," Todd said solemnly.

"You'd better stop watching that show," I scolded. "Stop reading the scary books and stop watching *The X-Files*, Todd. You're making yourself crazy."

"Look at this creepy house," Todd argued. "A house that looks like this *has* to be haunted. It has to —"

"Mom and Dad are really worried about you," I interrupted. "They think you're totally losing it."

"No way, I —" Todd started to protest.

But a deafening crash shook the house.

Todd and I both jumped and cried out. "What was *that*?"

"Downstairs!" I gasped.

We took off down the hall, floorboards creaking and groaning. I reached the stairs first and started down, leaning hard on the banister, taking the stairs two at a time.

Halfway down, I started into the living room — and saw what had caused the crash. A bookshelf had fallen off the wall. The bookshelf Dad just built last weekend.

It had toppled over into our couch. Books and framed photos and flower vases had spilled across the floor.

"What is it? What happened?" Todd came barreling down the stairs so fast, he bumped into me. I grabbed the railing to keep from tumbling the rest of the way down.

"Look out!" I growled. "It's just Dad's bookshelf."

Squeezing the banister with both hands, Todd leaned forward and stared into the living room. "That's just the kind of thing a ghost would do," he declared.

I turned to him. "Excuse me?"

"Ghosts always do mischief," he explained, his eyes on the fallen bookshelf. "A ghost did that, Mitchell. I know it!"

I groaned and rolled my eyes. "Todd, you're crazy," I replied through gritted teeth. "You know it wasn't a ghost. You know it has to be Dad's fault. Has Dad *ever* built a bookshelf that stayed on the wall for more than a week?"

"I heard that!" a voice cried.

Dad lumbered into the room, wiping his hands with a towel. I guessed he had been working on some project in the basement since his hands were smeared with grease and two of his fingers were cut.

He wore baggy, paint-stained jeans and an old white shirt with several buttons missing. The front of his shirt was also smeared with grease.

He brushed his straight brown hair off his forehead and stared at the fallen bookshelf, shaking his head. "Wrong brackets," he muttered to himself.

"Todd thought it was a ghost," I snitched.

Still wiping his hands, Dad turned to us on the stairway. "No. I used the wrong brackets," he said. "Todd, you've really got to stop seeing ghosts everywhere you look."

"Okay, Dad," Todd replied quickly. He never wants to argue with Dad. Dad has a bad temper, and Todd hates to be yelled at. "I'll try."

Dad gazed at Todd for a long moment. Then he stepped around the couch, grabbed the top of the bookshelf, and shoved it into a standing position. He leaned it carefully against the wall.

"Broke a vase and a few picture frames," he muttered unhappily. "Your mom won't be pleased."

Todd and I made our way down the stairs, into the living room. I bent down and picked some books off the floor and set them on the coffee table.

"Why don't you guys come with me to the hardware store?" Dad asked. "We'll buy the right brackets. You're not doing anything important, right?"

"Can I buy more glue and some fiberglass?" I asked. "Todd made me crack my Camaro model."

"It wasn't my fault!" Todd whined. "Why do I always have to be blamed for everything?"

"Calm down, guys," Dad said. "Get your jackets, and we'll go."

A few seconds later, we stepped outside. The rain had stopped, but heavy clouds floated low over the hill. Our front lawn glistened wetly. I could still hear raindrops falling from the trees.

Our front yard sloped down steeply toward the town. A misty gray fog covered the valley, blanketing the town from view.

The car was parked in the driveway. It was a fourteen-year-old Chrysler, puke green, a wreck of a car with rusted bumpers and one headlight cracked. Dad seldom bothered pulling it into the garage.

"When are we getting a new car?" I moaned, climbing into the front passenger seat.

Dad frowned. "Mitchell, do you have to ask that question every single time you get in the car?"

"I get to ride in front on the way home," Todd whined. He slammed the back door so hard, I thought the old car would fall apart.

Dad turned the ignition key and started pumping the gas pedal. The car started up with a groan on the third try. He let it warm up for a while, then backed down the drive.

"This car can barely start. Look how long it takes to warm up," I complained. "I've been reading the car ads, Dad. You don't have to buy a new car. You can lease one."

Dad rolled his eyes. "I don't want a new car," he replied through gritted teeth. "I take really good care of this car. It drives just fine."

He leaned over the wheel and guided the car around the curves. Forrest Valley Road slopes sharply, curving as it goes, down into the valley below.

Gray fog billowed around us as we rolled lower. Dad switched on the headlights. But they didn't help much. The fog reflected the light back onto the car.

"Can't see two feet ahead of me," Dad grumbled. He squinted straight ahead through the clouded windshield, both hands gripping the top of the wheel.

"Hey!" He uttered a sharp cry.

His foot started pumping, pumping hard up and down. His mouth dropped open. His face beamed bright red.

"Dad — what's wrong?" I cried.

He didn't reply. He pumped his foot frantically.

The car picked up speed, rolling down the hill faster, bouncing, shooting through the thick fog.

"No brakes!" Dad cried. "I don't believe it! No brakes!"

3

"Ohhhhh." A frightened moan escaped my throat.

The car bounced hard. Dad cut the wheel.

I fell against the door with a hard *THUD*.

I heard Todd whimpering in the back.

The steering wheel bounced under Dad's hands as if it were about to fly off.

I heard a loud roar. A car horn. We all screamed as a black van shot toward us from the wall of fog.

Dad spun the wheel. The car shuddered as the van roared past.

We rolled down the road. Faster. Faster.

The road dropped dangerously. Dad twisted the wheel, one way, then the other, struggling to see the curves through the heavy fog.

We bounced hard. I cried out as my head bumped the ceiling. The seat belt cut into my waist.

"We're going to crash! We're going to crash!" Todd wailed.

Dad's leg shot up and down as he pumped the brake. "Noooo!"

The car slid. We went into a skid.

Tires squealed.

I heard a car horn. A gray car roared past us.

We skidded off the road. Toward a forest of dark trees.

"Noooo!"

I saw Dad's right hand leave the bouncing steering wheel. He gripped the emergency brake and jerked it up.

I shut my eyes.

And rocked hard — forward then back — as the car hit.

I heard the crunch of metal. A crackling sound. Shattering glass.

My head hit the dashboard. Then I shot back up.

I heard Todd utter a high squeak.

Then silence.

I opened my eyes. Blinked several times. It took me a while to realize that the car had stopped.

We had hit a tree. Head-on. The windshield had cracked. Beyond it, I saw the hood crushed and mangled.

My heart raced in my chest. I could feel the blood pulsing at my temples.

"Are we . . . okay?" Dad's voice came out tiny, just above a whisper. Shaking his head as if to clear it, he turned to the back. "Todd?"

"I'm okay, Dad," Todd replied softly.

"Me, too," I said, trying to swallow. My mouth was suddenly as dry as sandpaper.

"I — I just fixed those brakes last week," Dad murmured. And then his expression changed. His eyes bulged. He tore off his seat belt. Shoved open the car door.

"Dad?" I called.

He lurched out of the car. Leaned over and started to puke. Loud, violent retching, his whole body heaving.

I waited until he stopped. Then I called out, "Does this mean we're getting a new car?"

I was already awake and dressed when the Sunday newspaper arrived the next morning. I lugged it inside and tossed aside all the sections until I found the car ads.

Then I spread the section out on the living room floor and began circling the ads that looked good. When Dad finally came down for breakfast at eight-thirty, still in his pajamas, I was ready for him.

"Check out this one," I said, shoving the paper in his face.

He blinked and brushed a tangle of dark hair from over his eye. "Mitchell — I'm still asleep." He groaned and rubbed his shoulder. "I'm a little sore, from the accident, I guess. How about you?"

"I'm fine. Check out this ad," I replied impatiently.

"Can't I have a cup of coffee first?" He groaned. "I can't focus. Really."

"Okay. I'll read it to you," I said.

I read him the ad: "*One owner, new model sports sedan. Perfect condition. V-8, white leather interior, all safety features. Owner must sell. Name your own price.*"

Dad squinted at me, rubbing his stubbly face. "What was that last line?"

"Name your own price," I repeated.

"That has to be a come-on," he muttered.

"Can we go see it?" I cried. "There's a phone number and an address here. It's on Wilbourne Street."

"In the valley. On the other side of town," Dad said.

"What are you two talking about?" Mom appeared at the top of the stairs. She tied the belt on her robe. "Mitchell, what are you doing up so early? Did you forget this is Sunday?"

"Dad and I are going to look at a car," I replied, grinning. "Right, Dad?"

After breakfast, Dad and I started down the hill toward town. Todd wanted to come, too, but he has karate lessons on Sunday.

Dad was driving a white Ford Taurus he rented

after the accident. "I kind of like this car," he said, smiling. "Good family car."

"But, Dad," I protested. "The car we're going to see sounds so *cool*."

The sun poked out between white snakes of clouds, sending streaks of light over the tall trees that lined the road. We made our way easily down to the valley this time and drove through town with only a few stops at traffic lights.

Town was nearly empty. Most of the stores are closed on Sunday morning. The only sign of life was the huge field behind the middle school where the soccer league games were under way, with hundreds of screaming kids, coaches, and parents.

"What was the address again?" Dad asked, slowing to pass three helmeted teenagers on bikes.

I pulled the ad from my pocket and read him the address again.

"It should be a few blocks from here," Dad said, turning onto a block of square white-shingled houses. "Now, listen, Mitchell. I have to warn you. We're just going to *look* at this car. I'm not going to whip out my checkbook and buy it on the spot. Do you understand?"

"But what if it's great?" I demanded. "What if it's totally perfect?"

"Listen to me," Dad said, slowing the car, squinting at the numbers on the mailboxes. "Read my lips, Mitchell. We're not buying today. We're only looking."

"But if it's the most awesome car we've ever seen?" I insisted.

He didn't reply.

He turned into a gravel driveway beside a small, square, white frame house. "This is it," he murmured. "The car must be in the garage in back." A garage, just a little smaller than the house, stood at the end of the driveway.

We made our way to the front stoop. The door was open. Dad knocked on the glass storm door.

I heard footsteps inside. A few seconds later, a tall, thin man wearing denim overalls and a red-and-black flannel shirt pushed open the storm door. He tilted his head and stared at us with tiny, round blue eyes.

He reminded me of an eagle or maybe a buzzard, with intense eyes, a broad forehead, and a long, crooked beak of a nose over a tiny O of a mouth. He kept those blue bird-eyes trained on us for the longest time.

Dad finally broke the silence. "Mr. Douglas? We called earlier. About the car?"

Mr. Douglas titled his head the other way. He nodded and cleared his throat. "It's around back. In the garage."

The aroma of frying bacon floated out from the house. I tried to see inside, but Mr. Douglas blocked the way. He stepped out onto the stoop and closed the storm door behind him.

"Nice morning," he muttered, scratching his

17

head of stringy brown hair as he stepped past us and started toward the garage.

"Yes. After all the rain," Dad replied. "This is Mitchell. He spotted your ad in the paper and —"

Mr. Douglas stopped in the driveway and turned to me. "Mitchell? You like cars?"

I nodded. "Yes. I like sports cars and vintage cars. I build models," I said.

He nodded. "Well . . . I think you'll like this car a lot, Mitchell."

We followed him along the driveway, our shoes crunching over the gravel. He stopped a few feet from the garage and began fumbling in his overalls pocket.

I let out a gasp and turned to Dad.

"The garage door," I murmured. "Why is it covered with padlocks?"

"The padlocks?" Mr. Douglas narrowed his bird-eyes at me.

I could feel myself blushing. I didn't mean for him to hear me.

"I have to keep the car locked up," he said, pulling a ring of keys from his pocket. "It's a pretty bad neighborhood. One of my neighbors had a car stolen just last week."

But so many *padlocks?* I thought. I counted six of them on the garage door.

It took him forever to find the right keys for the right locks and unlock them all. By the time he slid open the garage door, my heart was pounding with excitement.

As the door moved up, sunlight rolled over the car. The chrome bumper glowed like gold, reflecting the sun. The curved trunk shimmered, silvery in the spreading light.

"Wow!" I exclaimed.

Even from behind, the car was incredible!

"It has sports car designing," Mr. Douglas said, watching my reaction. "But it seats four."

"There are four in my family!" I declared.

The padlock keys jangled in Mr. Douglas's hand. He slid them back into his overalls pocket. "As you can see, there isn't a scratch on it," he told Dad. "And it has less than ten thousand miles. It's hardly been driven."

"It's incredible!" I exclaimed.

Dad frowned at me. "Easy, Mitchell," he warned.

Dad and I circled the car. I ran my hand over the smooth fenders. The car was all blue with a white leather interior. It was built low to the ground and looked as if it was speeding at ninety miles per hour even standing still!

It reminded me a lot of an old Corvette. It had the same sleek design, except it had a backseat.

"Wow!" I exclaimed again, peering in at all the dials and controls.

Dad chuckled. "I think Mitchell approves," he told Mr. Douglas.

Mr. Douglas swept a hand back through his stringy hair. His small mouth remained set in a tight *O*. He didn't smile. His eyes stayed on the car.

Dad stepped out of the garage. "Is there anything wrong with it?" he asked Mr. Douglas. "Why do you want to sell it?"

"Wrong with it?" Mr. Douglas tilted his head, his eyes thoughtful. "No. Nothing wrong with it. I . . . I have no use for it. That's all."

He turned away. I saw his hands tremble for just a second. He quickly shoved them into his overalls pockets.

Dad squatted down and examined the tires. "Like new," he murmured. He ran his hand over the silvery wheel cover.

"Want to take a test drive?" Mr. Douglas offered.

"Yes!" I cried.

Dad frowned at me again. He turned to Mr. Douglas. "Yes. Why don't you show us how it drives."

"Oh, no!" Mr. Douglas declared. He took a step back.

Why does he look frightened? I wondered.

He cleared his throat and began fumbling once again in his pockets. "No. I mean . . . uh . . . it would be better if you took the car out yourself."

He pulled the car keys out and shoved them at my dad. I saw that his hand was shaking. "Okay? I . . . I'll stay here. You give the car a try."

Dad squinted at him. "You sure you don't want to come along and show it off for us?"

Mr. Douglas pushed the keys into Dad's hand. "No. I . . . have some things to do around here. Uh . . . I haven't quite finished breakfast."

"Oh. I'm really sorry," Dad replied. "We didn't mean to interrupt. . . ."

"Take the car for a spin. Go ahead," Mr. Douglas insisted. "Just back it straight out of the garage.

I'll wait here. When you return, we can talk about price. I . . . I know you're going to want it. It's a wonderful car."

He turned and hurried to his house, taking long strides.

Dad and I watched him until he disappeared inside. "Weird," I muttered.

I opened the passenger door and lowered myself onto the soft leather seat. "Mmmmmm. Feels so good."

Dad slid behind the wheel. He adjusted his seat, then the mirror.

"Why does that man look so frightened?" I asked.

Dad shrugged. "Beats me." He pulled the seat belt over his shoulder. "I don't know what his problem is. But okay. Fine. We'll check out the car without him. What could happen?"

He slid the key into the ignition and turned it.

The car started right up. The engine hummed.

Dad lowered his foot on the gas pedal. The hum became a steady roar.

"Sounds good," Dad said. "Very clean." He grabbed the gearshift in his right hand and eased it into reverse. The car rolled out of the garage and down the gravel driveway.

I could see Mr. Douglas watching us from his front window. He gazed out at us with his hands in his pockets, standing still as a statue.

Dad shifted into drive, and we drove off. He turned at the corner, sped up, slowed down again, testing the brakes, then made a sharp right turn.

"It handles wonderfully," he commented. "This car practically drives itself."

"Let's buy it!" I cried.

"Whoa. Slow down." Dad laughed. "A car is a very important purchase, Mitchell," he scolded. "You don't just buy the first car you look at. Besides, I'm sure we can't afford this car. Mr. Douglas probably wants twenty or thirty thousand dollars for it."

"But the ad in the newspaper said —" I started.

"That doesn't mean anything," Dad replied. "This is a real luxury car, Mitchell. You know cars better than I do. You know a car like this is way beyond our budget."

I ran my hand over the smooth seat. "It sure is awesome," I muttered.

Dad turned on the radio. Music surrounded us from four speakers. He tested the turn signal, then the lights, then the heater and air conditioner.

"Everything is perfect," he said, turning back onto Wilbourne. "Wonder why Mr. Douglas wants to sell such a terrific car."

"Wonder why he wouldn't come with us," I added.

Dad eased the car up the gravel driveway. He stopped at the side of the house and turned off the engine.

"Just ask about the price," I urged. "It doesn't hurt to ask — right?"

Dad sighed. "I guess. But don't get your hopes up, Mitchell. This car is way beyond what I can afford."

I pushed open the car door, climbed out, and nearly bumped into Mr. Douglas. "Oh. Sorry," I murmured.

He gazed at me with those pale blue bird-eyes

but didn't say anything. He pulled a white handkerchief from his back pocket and mopped his forehead.

Why is he sweating? I wondered. *It's cold out today. I can see my breath.*

"You're back," he said finally, studying Dad.

Why does he appear so relieved to see us? I asked myself. *Didn't he think we were coming back?*

"Nice car," Dad said, patting the shiny blue roof. "Handles really well."

Mr. Douglas nodded. "You liked it? Good family car, right? Does your wife drive?"

"Yes," Dad replied. "I think she —"

"I can drive in four years!" I interrupted. "If I take drivers' ed. in school. I already know how. Dad let me take the wheel once when we were out in the desert in Arizona."

I expected Mr. Douglas to smile at that. But to my surprise, his chin quivered, and I saw tears form in his eyes.

He turned away and blew his nose into the handkerchief. "Must be getting a cold," he muttered.

"Well, I like the car," Dad said, scratching his thick, dark hair. "But we're looking for something a little less —"

"I'll give you a really good price," Mr. Douglas interrupted. He narrowed his eyes at the car and set his jaw in a cold scowl. "I really have to get rid of it."

His expression sent a chill down my spine.

Dad backed away from the car, shaking his head. "I don't think —"

"Would five thousand be too much?" Mr. Douglas asked.

Dad swallowed hard. "Five thousand? You mean as a down payment?"

"No. Five thousand total," Mr. Douglas replied. "It's a used car. Even though it's in perfect shape, I know I can't get full price for it. I'll sell it to you for five thousand."

"Dad —" I whispered, tugging his sleeve. "Do it!"

I wanted to cheer at the top of my lungs, pump my fists over my head, leap into the air.

Somehow I managed to stay on the ground.

"Well . . ." Dad rubbed his chin as if he was thinking it over. But I could see his eyes flashing excitely. I knew he was going to say yes!

"Are you sure there isn't anything wrong with it, Mr. Douglas?" he asked.

"Wrong with it?" Mr. Douglas tilted his head thoughtfully. "No. Nothing wrong with it. Nothing wrong with it at all."

But then his eyes clouded over. And his face darkened, as if a shadow had fallen over it. "But if you buy it," he said softly, "I have to ask you to do one thing."

"One thing?" Dad asked. "What is it?"

Mr. Douglas lowered his eyes to the car. "You have to drive it away immediately," he said. "You have to take it away *today*."

Dad and I exchanged glances.

This is one weird dude, I thought. I could see that Dad agreed.

"I have the registration and the bill of sale," Mr. Douglas said, nodding toward his house. "It's all ready. If you have your checkbook, I could bring it out and sign the car over to you."

"Uh ... well ..." Dad hesitated. He stared hard at me, then at the car. "Okay, Mr. Douglas. It's a deal."

"Yaaaaay!" I couldn't hold it in any longer. I let out a long cheer and jumped for joy.

Dad started to follow Mr. Douglas to the house, but the man waved Dad back. "I'll bring it out. No need to come inside." He disappeared into the house. The storm door slammed behind him.

"What a strange man," Dad murmured. "Why doesn't he want us to come inside?"

I was so excited, I felt about to burst. "Dad! It's ours! The car is ours! It — it's so totally awesome!"

I couldn't stay on the ground. I had to do something before I exploded!

I raised both hands above my head — and did a double cartwheel across the grass. But I misjudged the second cartwheel — pushed off a little too hard — and landed flat on my back.

"Ow!" I started laughing. I couldn't stop. I just sprawled on my back in the grass and laughed.

Dad laughed, too. "I'm excited," he confessed. "But I don't think I'll try any cartwheels."

He raced over and pulled me to my feet. "I think we made a really good deal, Mitchell," he said, grinning happily. "A really good deal."

At dinner that night, I smeared spaghetti sauce all over my face and spilled my juice. I couldn't help it. I was so excited about the car, I couldn't control myself.

"Dad, can we take a long drive after dinner?" I asked.

"Wipe your face," Mom replied. "Are you eating that spaghetti or wearing it?"

"Can we?" I repeated, swiping the napkin over my cheeks and chin.

"Mitchell, we took a long ride this afternoon," Dad said. "I have things I have to work on tonight. I know you love it, but we can't spend our whole life in that car."

"Mitchell wants to live in the car!" Todd exclaimed. Then he laughed his head off as if he'd made a really terrific joke.

"Maybe I *do* want to live in the car!" I shot back, leaning across the table at him. "So what?"

Todd grinned. "Where would you go to the bathroom?"

Dad laughed.

"That's not funny," Mom snapped. "Todd, we're at the dinner table, remember?"

"How about a short ride," I suggested. "Just down the hill to town and back?"

"No. You have homework," Mom replied sternly. "School tomorrow — remember?"

I tore off half a roll and shoved it into my mouth.

"We're all very excited about the new car," Mom said, passing the spaghetti bowl to Dad. "But, remember, we're going to have the car for a long, long time. And there will be plenty of time to ride in it."

"How about if I just sit in it?" I cried. "I just want to sit behind the wheel and maybe play the radio and try the headlights. Okay?"

"Not okay," Mom said, shaking her head. "Homework. No car. No more."

I knew better than to argue. When Mom starts talking in very short sentences, she means business.

The others kept talking as we finished dinner, but I didn't hear them. I kept thinking about the new car. About its silvery-blue exterior. The soft leather seats. The gentle, steady hum of its engine . . .

Later, I tried to do some homework. But I kept jumping up and going to my bedroom window, leaning out to peer down at the car. Dad had parked it in the driveway, and I could see it clearly since my room faces the front.

A streetlight sent a rectangle of yellow light over the car, making the chrome bumpers sparkle and the sleek blue body glow softly like moonlight.

I couldn't resist.

I had to go sit in the car.

I crept out into the hallway. I made sure Todd wasn't around. The little snitch would tell Mom and Dad.

I could hear music and gunfire and explosions from his room down the hall. I guessed he was in there playing video games.

I made my way silently down the stairs, leaning hard against the wall to keep the wooden steps from creaking. I could hear Mom talking on the phone from the den.

I stopped at the bottom of the stairs. Where was Dad?

"Ow!" I heard his angry cry from the back hall. I twisted around until I glimpsed him, on his knees on the floor, tools spread around.

He had an electrical cord raised in one hand. I guessed it was the cord he'd been working on before.

I heard a loud crackling sound. "Ow!" Dad cried out again. He dropped the cord and shook his hand furiously.

The cord definitely was not fixed.

Holding my breath, I turned and tiptoed to the front door. A few seconds later, I was outside. My sweatshirt fluttered in a strong, cold wind. A pale sliver of a moon faded behind wisps of black clouds.

I shivered. *Too late to go back for a coat. I'll be warm inside the car.*

I jogged along the walk to the driveway. The car shimmered in the light from the streetlamp.

I stepped around to the driver's side and grabbed the chrome handle.

"Go ahead," a voice whispered. *"Climb in."*

"Huh? Who said that?" I called out in a choked whisper.

I spun around. "Who's there? Todd?"

No. No one behind me. No one in the driveway.

I hurried around to the passenger side. No one hiding on the other side of the car.

As I made my way back to the driver's door, I heard the whispered voice again: *"Come in. Let's go."*

I hesitated with my hand on the door handle. I lowered my head and peered into the front seat.

"Is someone in there?"

No one.

Just my imagination, I thought.

I pulled open the door. It slid open so easily, I barely had to tug it. The ceiling light came on, making the creamy white seats glow.

I lowered myself behind the wheel and quickly pulled the door closed. I didn't want the ceiling light on. I didn't want anyone to see me from the house.

I settled into the seat and ran my hands over the steering wheel. Smooth and cool.

I gripped the gearshift at my side. I shifted from park to neutral, then back to park.

I leaned over the wheel and pretended to drive. I pushed down the turn signals. I shifted gears again.

I'm a race car driver, I decided. *Coming around the far turn. Passing the pack and moving into first.* I lowered my foot on the gas pedal.

Gun it, Mitchell. Gun it.

Take off!

I shifted again. Spun the wheel.

I'm going into a hairpin turn. Skidding. Sliding out of control.

Go with it! Go with it!

I spun the wheel into the skid. Regained control. Roared down the straightaway. I could see them waving the green flag, waving me in.

Victory!

The roar of the other engines, the cheers of the crowd — deafening. I decided to take the car around one more time in a victory lap.

I hit the brake when the porch light flashed on.

I gasped and grabbed the wheel tightly. I stared out the windshield at the cone of bright light that washed over the front stoop.

Who turned on the porch light? Mom? Dad? Were they going to come looking for me?

I'd better get out of the car, I decided.

I grabbed the door handle and tugged.

The door didn't open.

I tugged the handle again and leaned my shoulder against the car door.

No. It didn't budge.

Locked. *The door must have locked,* I realized.

I twisted around and searched for the little knob that unlocked the door.

No knob.

I slid my hand along the door, searching for the lock control.

How did I lock the doors? Do they lock automatically?

I couldn't find anything to unlock the door. I grabbed the handle again. Tried pushing it down. But it didn't go that way.

I yanked the handle up. Yanked it hard this time. And shoved all my weight against the door.

No. No go.

"Hey — how do I get *out* of here?" I cried out loud.

I hit the window control. Pressed it, trying to lower the electric power windows.

But they didn't work with the engine turned off.

"Hey!"

I tried the handle one more time. I pushed at the door. I slapped it with both hands.

34

I'm locked in. Locked in.

My heart pounding, I fumbled for a lock control again.

I stopped when I heard the laughter.

Soft, high laughter. A girl's laughter.

"Hey — who's there?" I called breathlessly.

The laughing continued, soft but cold.

"Who's laughing?"

I turned my head to the driver's window. Stared out into the darkness — and saw a face staring in at me.

A girl.

She had wavy blond hair that caught the light from the streetlamp. Dark, catlike eyes. She stared in at me as if I were a Martian!

"Pull the door!" I instructed, motioning frantically to the outside handle. "It's stuck!"

She nodded and grabbed the handle.

The car door swung open.

She took a step back as I leaped out of the car, breathing hard.

"Are you okay?" she asked. She had a low, whispery voice. "What were you doing in there?"

"The . . . the lock was stuck," I stammered. I brushed a strand of hair from over my eye and studied her.

She wore a blue down vest, open over a dark V-neck sweater. Her straight-legged jeans were torn at one knee. When she brushed back her shoulder-length hair, I saw that she had three different earrings jangling from each ear.

"It's a new car," I explained. "I mean, we just bought it this morning."

She nodded. A smile spread over her face, revealing a dimple in each cheek.

She's really great-looking, I decided. *She looks like a model or a TV star.*

"You were trying it out?" she asked in that soft, purring voice.

I nodded. "Yeah. I . . . like cars."

She rested her hand on the fender. Her nails were shiny blue, and she had two or three rings on each finger.

"I saw you were having trouble," she said. "It's a good thing I came by, huh?"

"For sure," I agreed. "Thanks." And then I added, "Who are you?"

For some reason, my question made her laugh. "My name is Marissa Meddin," she announced.

I told her my name.

"This is my new neighborhood," she said, sliding her hand back and forth over the car fender as if petting it. "I was taking a walk. You know. Checking it out."

"You just moved here?" I asked. Stupid question. She already told me it was her new neighborhood. "Which house?"

She pointed with her head. Toward the old Faulkner house just past the corner.

That old dump? I thought. *No one has lived in that house for years.*

"Are you going to go to Forrest Valley Middle School in town?" I asked.

"Probably," she replied, making a sour face. "I don't know yet. I hate transferring to a new school after the year has already started."

"Where did you live before?" I asked.

"Somewhere else," she replied, and giggled.

"No. Really," I insisted. "Did you move —"

I stopped and uttered a startled cry as someone bumped me from behind.

I spun around. "Todd!"

He grinned up at me.

"What are *you* doing out here?" I demanded.

"What are *you* doing out here?" he mimicked. "You sneaked out — didn't you, Mitchell! To sit in the car. I'm telling. I'm telling right now!"

"No — wait!" I cried.

"I'm telling — unless I can sit in the driver's seat for a while," Todd declared. He made a move toward the car, but I pulled him back.

"No way," I told him. "Stay away from the new car. You'll get us both in major trouble."

"Then I'm telling!" he whined.

I held him by his skinny shoulders. "Listen to me, Todd. You can't sit in the car. The car doors are sticking. They —"

"Liar!" he cried.

"No. Really," I insisted. "I was locked in. If Marissa hadn't opened the door, I would have been locked inside all night."

"Who?" Todd demanded.

"Marissa," I told him.

I whirled around. "Marissa?"

She had vanished.

Todd gave me a hard shove. "Liar!" he growled.

"Shhhh. Quiet!" I cried, raising a finger to my lips. I glanced toward the doorway. "We're supposed to be inside. We don't want Mom and Dad to catch us out here."

Todd crossed his arms over the front of his fake leather bomber jacket. "When do I get to sit in the car?"

"Tomorrow. I promise," I whispered. "Now, come on."

I took his hand and led him to the front stoop. I pushed open the front door and cautiously peered inside.

No sign of Mom or Dad.

I could hear voices on the TV from the den.

"Hurry," I whispered.

We crept inside, and I carefully closed the door behind us. I motioned to the stairs across the hall.

We were almost there when I heard the loud cry from the back hallway.

I rushed forward in time to see a blinding flash of white light.

And an eerie figure inside the light, staggering toward us, trembling arms raised high.

"That's it!" Todd wailed. "That's the *ghost*!"

"Whoooooaaah!" Surrounded by crackling white light, the figure uttered a terrifying moan as it staggered toward us.

"Todd — it's not a ghost!" I shrieked. "It's *Dad*!"

Dad gripped the electrical cord in one hand. His arms shot up and down. His hair stood straight up on his head.

"He's being electrocuted!" I screamed.

I dove down the hall. I spotted a pair of his rubber work gloves on the floor beside him.

The white burst of electricity sizzled and jumped around him.

I grabbed one of the gloves and frantically pulled it onto my hand. Then I leaped to the wall. Found the end of the cord.

Ripped the plug out.

Silence. And then a heavy *THUD* as Dad dropped to the floor.

He groaned.

I spun around. He sank to his hands and knees. His hair still stood straight up. His face was tomato-red. His lips were purple.

"Dad!" I gasped. I tossed the rubber glove away and stumbled over to him.

Todd had his face covered with both hands. His entire body shuddered.

Dad's eyes bulged. He opened his mouth to speak, but only a few weak grunts came out. "Unh . . . unh . . ."

"Dad? Are you okay?"

The air smelled smoky, as if there had been a fire.

I heard rapid footsteps. Mom burst into the hall. Her mouth dropped open as she spotted Dad on all fours. "Huh? Oh, my goodness! What happened?"

Dad took a deep breath. He pulled himself up to a sitting position and shrugged. "Guess this cord isn't quite fixed," he said softly.

That night, I dreamed about the new car.

At first, I saw it surrounded in the glow of crackling electricity. I stood outside it. Reached out for the door handle.

But a hard jolt of electricity sent me staggering back.

I tried again. Slowly, slowly, reached out my hand to the chrome handle.

And again, a sizzling shock made me reel backward. Pain shot through my hand, my arm, my whole body.

I woke up.

I was lying on my side, my arm buried beneath me. It tingled and ached. My arm had fallen asleep.

I rolled onto my back and shook my arm until the tingling stopped. It didn't take long to fall back to sleep.

I dreamed again about the car.

This time, I sat behind the wheel. At first, I thought the car was flying. It glided along so smoothly.

But then I saw dark trees rushing by.

I leaned over the wheel, gazing into the twin white beams from the headlights, guiding the car easily. I lowered my foot to the gas pedal.

With a soft hum, the car sped up. The trees whirred past on both sides.

The headlights cut through the darkness. I moved the wheel between my hands, following the gentle curve of the road.

Faster.

The engine hum grew to a low roar.

The passing trees became a blur of black against the gray sky.

The steering wheel bounced in my hands. I gripped it tighter.

I raised my foot from the gas pedal.

But the car sped up.

Faster. Faster now.

The road swept right, then sharply left. I spun the wheel, frantically trying to stay on the pavement.

Faster.

I could see only whirring darkness now. The trees, the sky, the black road ahead — all melted into a shadow that I was diving through. Plunging faster, faster.

And then a blinding white light made me pull one hand off the bouncing wheel to shield my eyes.

Headlights.

A car roaring toward me — on my side of the street!

And behind the wheel of the other car — Marissa. I could see her so clearly. See her blond hair bouncing behind her. See the strange grin on her face.

"Marissa — no! No!"

I spun the wheel. Desperately struggled to pull away.

But she was coming right at me.

"Marissa — no!" I shrieked at the top of my lungs. *"We're going to crash!"*

I woke up drenched in sweat.

My blanket and sheet were tangled around my legs. My pajama shirt was twisted around my neck, choking me.

I sat up shakily.

The white light of the headlights lingered in my eyes. I blinked several times, trying to blink the light away.

Finally, the dream faded. I gazed into orange morning sunlight streaming through my window.

"Whoa," I murmured, shaking my head. "What a dream."

Wiping the cold sweat off the back of my neck, I climbed out of bed. My legs felt shaky and weak. "What a dream," I repeated.

At breakfast a few minutes later, I described the dream to Todd. I had to tell *someone* about it.

"Who is Marissa?" he asked, chewing a mouthful of Frosted Flakes.

"I *told* you," I snapped. "The girl who let me out of the car last night."

"I didn't see any girl," he said. He had milk running down his chin.

"So?" I replied.

He dropped his spoon into the cereal bowl and narrowed his eyes at me. "Do dreams ever come true?" he asked.

"I guess," I replied. I tilted my glass over my mouth and downed the rest of my orange juice. No pulp. The kind I like.

"You mean *that* dream could come true?"

"No way," I told him. "How could it? I'm not old enough to drive, remember?"

"Maybe it was a warning," Todd murmured, spooning up some more cereal.

"Huh? What kind of warning?" I demanded. I was sorry I told him about the dream. I could see it upset him.

He shrugged. More milk dribbled down his chin.

"Why can't you work a spoon?" I sneered. "It really isn't that hard. Or do you have a hole in your chin?"

I laughed.

He opened his mouth wide and stuck out his tongue so I could see the clump of chewed-up cereal inside.

He's so gross.

"What happens if you die in a dream?" he asked.

His question caught me by surprise. I just stared across the table at him, trying to figure out what he meant.

"What if your car crashed in the dream? What if you and this girl really smashed into each other, and you died? Would you die in real life?"

"Huh?" I frowned at him. "No. I don't think so. It's just a dream — right? You can't die from a dream. At least, I don't *think* you can."

I jumped up from the table. "Todd, I'm sorry," I said. "Don't be upset. I shouldn't have told you about it. It was just a stupid dream, okay?"

"Okay," he murmured softly. But I could see he was thinking hard.

"Almost time to leave," I said, glancing at the kitchen clock. "Do you have your shoes on?"

He never has his shoes on. I always have to wait for him.

Todd's frightened questions repeated in my mind. *What if the dream was a warning? What if you crashed?*

I thought about the new car. I'd been awake for nearly an hour, and I hadn't even looked at it yet!

I hurried to the front window. Peered out into the bright morning sunlight — and gasped.

The car was gone.

"Mitchell, what's wrong?"

Mom hurried into the living room, buttoning her coat.

"The car —" I choked out, pointing to the driveway.

"Your father took it this morning. He had an early meeting," Mom reported. "Mrs. O'Connor is going to give us all a lift."

I breathed a sigh of relief. But I still felt disappointed.

After my scary dream, I wanted to see the car and make sure it was okay. And I wanted to ride in it to school and show it off to my friends.

I thought about the car all day. I don't think I heard a word Miss Grimm, my teacher, said.

Just before the final bell rang, I looked up from my seat to see Miss Grimm frowning down at me. She had her arms crossed tightly in front of her and was tapping one shoe against the floor.

"Mitchell — can you explain that?" she asked. She pointed down to the paper in front of me.

"Huh?" I glanced down at my history notes. And uttered a cry of surprise.

No notes. No words at all.

Instead, I had drawn the new car. I had drawn it over and over, at least twenty times — *without even realizing it.*

How did this happen? I wondered.

How could my hand draw these sketches completely on its own?

"Please, Dad — just a short ride! Please?"

I didn't like to beg. But he had already refused three or four times. So what choice did I have?

"Can't we finish our dinner in peace?" Mom groaned. She slammed her fork and knife onto the table.

"I don't really want to take you for a ride tonight, Mitchell," Dad said patiently. "It's going to rain and —"

"And Todd is running a little fever," Mom added.

"So he can stay home," I said.

"I have to stay home with him," Mom replied. "So —"

"So, it's just you and me, Dad!" I cried. "How about it? Just to town and back? Maybe we could pick up some aspirin for Todd or something."

Dad laughed. "Todd doesn't need aspirin." He

dabbed the napkin over his mouth. "But we do need milk," he added.

"And ice cream," Todd added hoarsely. "Ice cream for my sore throat."

"Okay, okay." Dad stood up, pushed his chair back, and stretched. "Mitchell and I are taking a short ride in the new car to town."

"YAAAAAY!" I cheered, shooting my fists into the air. I gulped down the rest of my milk and ran to get my jacket.

Dark clouds hung low in the sky, blocking the moon and stars. A low fog clung to the ground as Dad followed the curving road down the hill toward town. A few raindrops splashed the windshield.

"Look, Mitchell." Dad took his right hand off the wheel and steered with two fingers of his left hand. "The power steering is so delicate on this car, you barely have to touch the wheel to have total control."

"Awesome," I murmured. "It's a great car, isn't it, Dad?"

He nodded, a smile spreading over his face. "Yes. Great. And a real bargain!"

We didn't have any trouble until the trip back from town.

The rain started pounding down really hard. Sheets of rain thundered over the windshield, blurring the light from the headlights, making it impossible to see.

"It's like driving underwater," Dad muttered, slowing the car. Leaning over the wheel, he steered with his left hand. His right hand fumbled over the dashboard.

"I can't find the wipers," he scowled. "Do you see the wiper control?"

I leaned forward as far as the seat belt would allow me. I squinted at the dashboard. Radio . . . heater . . . flash signal . . .

"No. I don't see it, Dad."

Dad uttered a frustrated sigh. He pulled the car to the side of the road.

Rain washed over the car like ocean waves, one wave right after another.

"Quick — open the glove compartment," Dad ordered. "Find the manual. It will tell us where to find the wiper control. Hurry."

He continued to search the dashboard. "Where is it? Where is the stupid knob?"

Dad hates things like this. He always loses it in an emergency.

"I'll find it," I assured him. I pulled down the lid to the glove compartment. A tiny light flashed on.

I lowered my head and peered inside.

"Hey!" I cried out in surprise. No car manual in there. Nothing. Empty.

Except for a torn scrap of white paper.

"What is it?" Dad demanded, still searching the dashboard.

I pulled the scrap of paper from the glove compartment and, holding it in the dim light, read the scrawled words.

Two words: I'M EVIL.

I'M EVIL.

I read the words to Dad.

"What kind of stupid joke is that?" he growled.

Rain pelted the car. A heavy, dark wave washed over us. The car rocked under the weight of it.

Dad let out a cry. I heard a scraping sound and saw the wiper blades begin to slide over the windshield. Beyond the windshield, I could see the yellow blur of our headlights.

"I found it!" Dad exclaimed. "Stupid control is on the steering wheel shaft."

The wipers slid slowly up, then back, clearing the glass for only a second before the rain covered it again.

We waited by the side of the road for a while, listening to the steady roar of the rain, watching the wipers push the water away. Finally, the rain slowed enough to see clearly. Dad shifted into drive and guided the car back onto the road.

"Some storm," he muttered as we followed the curving road up the hill toward home.

"Yeah. Some storm," I repeated.

But I wasn't thinking about the rain. I held the scrap of paper in my hand and stared down at it the whole way back.

I'M EVIL.

Why would someone write that? Why was it left in our glove compartment?

My friends Allan and Steve dropped by the next night after dinner. I was in my room sketching the new car. I planned to design my own model of it and then build it.

"Bet you ten bucks Mitchell is drawing a car," I heard Allan say from out in the hall.

"No bet," Steve replied. "That's a sucker bet."

They were always betting each other on everything.

They burst into the room and laughed when they saw me hunched over my drawing.

They're both big guys, taller than me and athletic-looking, with broad necks like football players. Allan has curly red hair and a lot of freckles. Mom says he looks like the all-American boy, whatever that means.

Steve has black hair, shaved really short, and wears a silver ring in one ear.

"What are you guys doing here?" I asked, setting down my pen.

"You've been talking nonstop about your awesome new car," Allan replied. "So we came to check it out."

Steve grinned. "You have the keys, Mitchell? You want to take us for a ride?"

"Ha-ha," I said, rolling my eyes. "You're a riot."

"You told us your dad let you drive," Steve insisted, picking up my car drawing and studying it.

"Yeah, last summer. But that was way out in the desert in Arizona, and there wasn't another car around for a hundred miles," I replied.

He set the drawing back on the desk and pulled my arm. "Come on. Show us the car."

I led the way to the stairs. Of course, we bumped into Todd. When my friends come over, Todd always manages to be around.

"Where are you going?" he demanded, blocking the stairway.

"To Brazil," Allan joked. "Get out of the way, or we'll miss our plane."

"Take me with you," Todd insisted, crossing his scrawny arms over his scrawny chest.

"Why do you want to go to Brazil?" Allan asked him.

"You're not going to Brazil. You're going to check out the new car," Todd replied.

"Okay, okay, you can come." I sighed. I knew if I didn't agree, he'd come anyway.

I grabbed a jacket and we stepped outside. It was a cool, cloudy night. The ground was still wet from the heavy rains the night before.

Allan and Steve ran past me to the car parked near the bottom of the driveway. Light from the streetlamp poured over it, making the blue finish gleam.

"Way cool!" Allan declared.

Steve ran his hand over the hood, then bent down to examine the headlight covers. "It's built so low," he commented. "Like a race car."

"It sounds like a race car, too," I told him. "It has a V-8 that roars when you floor the gas."

"Cool," he murmured. He stood up. "Can we get inside?"

"Yeah. Why not?" I replied.

I grabbed the handle on the driver's side and pulled open the door. The memory of the lock sticking flashed into my mind.

But it hadn't happened again, so I didn't worry about it. Dad probably had everything fixed at the garage.

I slid behind the wheel. Allan climbed in beside me. Todd and Steve piled into the back. We closed all the doors.

"Mmmm. Real leather seats," Steve declared.

"Crank up the radio," Allan demanded.

"I can't," I told him. "I didn't bring the key."

"Well, go get it," Allan insisted.

"I don't think Dad would like it," I said. "He says if you sit in a car with the radio on, it wears down the battery."

I heard the door locks click.

The sound made me jump.

I turned to Allan beside me. "Did you hit the lock control on your door?"

He shook his head. "No way."

I shivered.

"Hey — it's getting cold in here!" Todd whined.

He was right.

I could see my breath steaming toward the windshield. I shivered again and zipped my jacket up all the way.

I felt a wave of cold air sweep over me. And then another blast, even colder.

"Hey, Mitchell, turn off the AC," Steve called, leaning over the seat. "It's freezing in here."

Shivering, I turned back to him. "The air conditioning isn't on. I told you, I don't have the key."

"I'm f-f-freezing," Todd stuttered.

I stared at the windshield. The glass was icing up on the inside!

It's not a normal cold, I realized. *It's such a heavy, deep cold. Where is it coming from?*

"This is totally weird," Allan murmured beside me.

"I'm getting out," Todd declared from behind me. "My face — it's freezing off!"

I heard him tug the door handle. And then I heard him cry out. "Hey — it's locked. Mitchell — unlock the door."

I tried my door. Locked.

Once again, I searched for the lock control.

"It's s-so c-cold!" I heard Steve stammer. "Mitchell — come on. Open the doors."

"I'm trying," I told him. My hand fumbled over the door controls searching for the right button.

The air grew colder. I rubbed my nose and ears. They were numb. My nostrils hurt when I breathed in.

So cold . . .

My chest ached. It suddenly felt tight. I struggled to breathe, but it made my chest throb with pain.

The cold is shutting off my air, I realized. Each breath made a high, wheezing sound.

My chest throbbed. I couldn't stop shivering.

I tried the door again. But my numb fingers wouldn't bend. I couldn't grab the handle.

Frantic, choked with panic, I shoved my shoulder against it. No.

It wouldn't budge.

And then I heard laughter. Very faint. A girl's laughter. Soft and . . . cruel.

Mean laughter.

The air grew even colder. I choked. Struggled to draw in a breath. But I couldn't.

Did my lungs freeze?

57

"Let us out!" Todd shrieked.

"Let us out of here!" Steve screamed.

We were all pounding on the doors and windows.

"Let us out! Somebody — let us out!"

13

My door flew open.

I toppled out. Shivering, my whole body shaking from the cold, I landed on my side on the driveway.

And stared up at Marissa.

Marissa pulled open a back door, and Todd and Steve burst out. Hugging themselves, they began hopping up and down, trying to warm up. A second later, Allan slid out through the open driver's door and joined them.

I climbed to my feet, forcing myself to stop shivering. The night air felt balmy and warm compared to the inside of the car.

"What's going on?" Marissa asked, turning from me to the others. "What is wrong with you guys?"

"F-f-freezing," Steve choked out.

"I'm going in," Todd announced. "Got to get warm!" He took off in a run and vanished into the house.

Marissa eyed me. "Mitchell, were you locked in again?"

"Yeah. We were locked in," Steve growled, answering for me. "And the dumb cluck had the air conditioner on!"

"I did not!" I cried.

"Funny joke, Mitchell," Allan muttered. "Real funny."

Steve gave me a shove. "You've got a weird sense of humor."

"Come on, guys —" I pleaded. "You've got to believe me. I didn't —"

But they took off, running along the street, toward their houses.

I watched them until they disappeared into the next block. Then I turned back to Marissa. "Lucky you came along again," I said.

"Yeah. I guess so," she replied, still studying me. "You really should get those doors fixed."

"I thought my dad had them fixed at the garage," I told her.

As I talked to Marissa, I was thinking about the laughter I'd heard inside the car. The girl's soft, cruel laughter.

Laughter as cold as the air in the car.

"I'm afraid to tell Dad about the doors," I said. "He might try to fix them himself." I shook my head. "If he does, he'll only make them worse."

"But you can't leave them like this," she insisted,

her eyes locked on mine. "It's dangerous, Mitchell. It's really dangerous."

It was nearly midnight, but I couldn't get to sleep.

Mom and Dad had gone to bed at eleven. The house was quiet and still. Gusts of wind rattled the old windowpanes in my bedroom window.

In my pajamas, I leaned on the windowsill and gazed down at the car at the bottom of the driveway. It suddenly looked to me like a leopard about to pounce.

I felt a hand on my shoulder.

I screamed — and spun around.

"Todd — what are you doing in here? Why are you still up?" I demanded.

He didn't reply. In the light from the street, I could see his face, tight with fear.

He stepped beside me and gazed down at the car.

"It's haunted," Todd whispered.

"What?"

"The car is haunted," he said.

I groaned. "Todd — please don't start with that ghost stuff again."

"It's haunted," he repeated, leaning on the windowsill and staring down at the car. His entire body shuddered. He turned to me. "I heard that girl laughing, Mitchell."

My mouth dropped open. "You heard it, too?"

He nodded.

"It might have been Marissa from outside the car," I said softly.

"Maybe," he replied. "But somebody locked those doors. Somebody locked us in and then made it cold."

"Todd —"

"It was a ghost!" he declared, his voice trembling, his face so pale in the gray light from outside. "I know it was a ghost. The car is haunted, Mitchell."

He was trembling. I put my hands gently on his shoulders. "That's crazy, Todd," I whispered. "You've got to stop imagining ghosts all the time."

"But — but —" he sputtered.

"The car needs work, that's all," I assured him. "It's a used car. It just needs a little work."

We talked a while longer. I think I calmed him down. He said good night and padded back to his room.

I started to bed. Stopped halfway across the floor.

Something pulled me back to the window. I had to see the car one more time.

Heavy black clouds floated low over the hill. The moon and stars were covered behind a blanket of darkness.

I peered down to the driveway — and gasped in surprise.

The car was bathed in an eerie green glow.

The pale green light circled the car, shimmered around it, growing brighter, brighter, then fading.

Then brighter again.

Pulsing.

What is doing that? I wondered. I stared down through the window, my forehead pressing against the cold pane.

Is Todd right? Is the car really haunted?

I turned from the window and grabbed my clothes.

I had to find out.

I made my way down the stairs, carrying my shoes. If Mom and Dad heard the steps creaking, I'd be caught. And how could I explain why I was sneaking out in the middle of the night?

I sat down in the hallway and pulled on my sneakers. I didn't bother to tie them. I wanted to get out to the car before that strange green glow disappeared.

I could hear the wind whistling through the living room windows. The old glass panes rattled. It sounded as if someone were shaking the house.

No wonder poor Todd thought the place was haunted!

Dad planned to replace the old window frames. But he hadn't had time. When it got really windy, we had to wear sweaters or coats inside the house.

I pulled on my down jacket. The car keys rested on the little table beside the front door. I picked them up and tucked them into my coat pocket. Then I carefully slid the front door open and slipped outside.

A strong blast of wind blew me back against the door. My hair flew into my eyes. I fumbled with my jacket zipper and finally managed to zip it up to the collar.

The night dew had frozen, leaving a thin layer of frost over the front lawn. Slipping and sliding, I jogged across the grass to the driveway.

The car no longer glowed.

It sat under the light from the streetlamp, shimmering and still. I ran up to the driver's door, my breath rising in front of me in puffs of white steam.

I peered into the frosted window. Dark inside the car.

Dark and empty.

I ran my hand over the roof.

Why isn't it glowing? I wondered. *Was that some kind of optical illusion, a trick of the light from my upstairs window?*

I felt disappointed.

The car held a mystery, and I wanted to solve it.

But here I was, out in the cold, windy night, standing in the driveway, staring at an empty car.

"Mitchell, you're acting like a jerk," I scolded myself. Shaking my head, I turned and started trudging back to the house.

I had walked only a step or two when I heard the soft voice: *"Climb in. Come on — get in."*

"Huh?" I let out a startled cry — and spun around so hard, my feet nearly slid out from under me on the frost-covered driveway.

"Get in. Hurry. Climb in."

I moved back to the car, leaning into another strong blast of wind. "Who are you?" I called. "Where are you?" My muffled voice blew back in my face.

Silence now. Except for the rush of wind through the nearly bare trees. Dead brown leaves swirled at my feet, spun around my legs as if trying to hold me back.

But I grabbed the door handle. "Who are you?" I repeated.

Cold fear made my whole body shudder. I knew I shouldn't obey the voice. I knew I should stay out of the car.

I remembered the locked doors, the frigid air, the cold, cruel laughter.

But I had sneaked outside to solve the mystery. And I couldn't solve it standing out here, shivering, staring into an empty car.

I pulled open the door and slid behind the wheel.

The leather seat was so cold, it stung my skin through my clothes. My breath steamed the windshield. I rubbed my hands over the cold, smooth steering wheel.

"Are you in here?" I whispered, turning, searching around. "Is someone in here?"

I listened for the girl's soft voice.

Silence.

"Mitchell, you're an idiot," I murmured out loud.

I was falling for my brother's stupid ghost talk. "Yeah, right," I told myself, rolling my eyes. "You're sitting in a haunted car."

The furious wind sent a clump of dead leaves scuttling over the windshield. Startled, I raised my hands as if to shield myself.

The leaves pressed flat against the glass as if pushing to get inside. Another wind gust carried them away.

"Is anyone in here?" I tried again. "Did someone call me?"

Silence.

Shivering, I shoved my hands into my coat pockets. And felt the car keys.

I pulled them out and stared at them. Why did I bring them with me? Did I plan to start the car?

No. Of course not.

I picked them up because it's the middle of the night and I am half asleep and not thinking clearly *and going crazy because there's something strange about this car that I can't figure out!*

I slipped the key into the ignition and turned it

one notch. It didn't start the engine. You have to turn the key all the way to start the engine.

"What am I doing?" I asked myself.

I knew I shouldn't be out here. I should be up in my bed, safe and warm and asleep.

But I couldn't stop myself.

I had a terrifying feeling. A feeling that some strange, invisible force had pulled me into the car. Had forced me to slide the key into the ignition. Had forced me to turn the key.

And then, I felt a rush of cold air as my hand shot out — and clicked on the radio.

I expected a blast of music. But instead, I heard the crackle and whistle of static.

I pushed a button. Then another.

No. No music.

Was the radio broken?

I spun the volume knob, turned it all the way up.

And the voice — the soft, girl's voice — whispered from the speakers: *"I'm evil . . . I'm so evil . . ."*

I opened my mouth to call out to her — but only a choked gurgle escaped my throat.

"I'm so evil . . ."

Before I could utter a sound, the engine started up. The headlights flashed on. The car shifted into reverse.

"Noooo!" I wailed. "This isn't happening! This *can't* be happening!"

But with a jolt that sent my head crashing against the windshield, the car shot back, down the driveway, into the street.

"Hey!" I shrieked. "Stop this! Let me out! Stop! *Let me out!*"

The car shot rapidly into the street.

As if pushed by an invisible hand, the gearshift moved to drive.

"Stop! What's happening?" I shrieked.

I grabbed the door handle. Tugged it up and shoved all my weight against the door.

Locked. Locked tight.

"Let me out!"

The tires skidded over the slick, frosty pavement. The car bolted forward, heading down the hill, down Forrest Valley Road.

"No! This is crazy! Who are you? What are you doing?"

I frantically tried the door again. It didn't open.

The car slid on the pavement. Picked up speed as it curved downhill.

I grabbed the steering wheel, struggling to keep the car on the road.

Gasping in panic, I slammed my foot down on the brake pedal.

But the car sped up instead of slowing to a stop.

Laughter poured from the radio speakers. The same low, cold laughter as before.

"Who are you? Where are you?" I screamed.

I tromped on the brake again, but the car didn't slow.

I grabbed the key in the ignition — and twisted it to off.

But the engine roared even louder.

I pulled the key from the ignition and jammed it in my coat pocket.

But the car rolled even faster.

"Noooo!" I uttered a terrified cry as the car swerved off the road, tires skidding. My head hit the ceiling as the car bumped over the hard ground.

I grabbed the wheel in both hands. Leaned over it. Spun it hard.

Guided the car back onto the road.

The road sloped steeply downhill. The buildings of town came into view, far below us.

I pumped the brake. I tried to shift into park.

I tugged on the emergency brake.

But the car rolled faster, faster, engine roaring.

"Enjoying the ride?"

The girl's voice floated from the speakers, so soft I could barely hear her over the roar of the engine, the rumble of the tires.

"Are you? Are you enjoying it?"

"Stop it! Stop the car — please!" I choked out. The wheel bounced in my hands. I spun it hard, struggling to follow the curves as we shot down the steep slopes.

I heard a long, low whistle. From somewhere far in the distance.

A train whistle?

The girl's laughter drowned out the sound.

"Who are you? Where are you?" I demanded, gripping the wheel, working it between both hands.

Despite the cold of the night, sweat poured down my forehead. My clammy hands slid on the steering wheel.

"But you like to drive!" the voice insisted, teasing, so cruel.

"No! No, I don't!" I wailed. "Stop the car. We're going to crash! Stop it now!"

"Stop it? Okay," she purred.

I felt the brake pedal slam down to the floor — and stay there.

I heard the tires squeal.

The car skidded — slid wildly out of control.

I spun the wheel, but it didn't help.

I cried out as the car began to spin.

Tires shrieking in protest, the car slid off the road.

Bumped over grass and shrubs. Bounced and skidded.

Toward the tall, dark trees beyond the shoulder.

The girl's laughter rose up from the speakers, rose up all around me as the trees loomed close.

I'm going to crash, I realized in those few fast seconds.

The laughter rang in my ears. Rang and echoed as if it were inside my head.

I'm going to crash.

I'm going to die.

I jerked the wheel hard, frantically trying to spin the car away from the trees.

The car bounced hard.

"Oww!" I cried out as my head shot up against the roof again.

The dark trees rose up in the windshield. The tires scraped over tall grass and weeds.

"Yes!" I spun the wheel again, and the trees slid out of view. The car whirled around, rocked up and down, faced the road once again.

Another hard bump. And then I was back on the pavement.

Roaring along the dark, curving street. Picking up speed.

"Stop the car! Stop it!" I screamed, the wheel jerking and twisting under my hands.

The girl's laughter floated over the roar of the engine.

In the distance, I heard the wail of the train whistle once again.

"Who are you? Why are you doing this?" I demanded, my voice bouncing with the car.

More cold laughter. And then she moaned, *"I'm evil . . . I'm so evil."*

And the train crossing came into view in the headlight beams.

I saw the guardrails slide down. Red lights flashed.

To the left, I could see the dark outline of the train, black against the purple night sky. A whir of motion as the engine approached the crossing.

I heard another long, low train whistle.

I slammed my foot down hard on the brake.

But the car shot forward.

The guardrails shone in the headlights as the car roared to the tracks.

"Good-bye, Mitchell." The girl's voice purred from the speakers. *"Hope you enjoyed your ride. Your last ride."*

Twin headlights from the front of the train poured over the crossing just a few yards in front of me. Bright white light that made me shield my eyes.

And scream louder than I've ever screamed.

My scream rose over the shriek of the train engine.

My breath cut off as the car braked with a hard jolt.

"Oooohhh!" I tossed forward over the wheel.

Then I rocked back hard against the seat.

The tires squealed as if crying.

The front bumper cracked into the wooden guardrails. The car bounced to a stop.

The train roared past.

I stared at the whir of train cars, gasping, my chest heaving up and down, struggling to catch my breath. My throat was raw from screaming. Chill after chill made my whole body shudder.

The train clattered past. It gave another long, low whistle blast, this one fading into the distance.

Silence now. Except for my rapid, shallow breaths and the thudding of my heart.

The car slowly backed up, away from the guardrails.

"Wasn't that fun?" the girl's voice whispered from the radio speakers. *"Did that give you a thrill?"*

"No!" I cried angrily. "Are you crazy?"

With a furious growl, I snapped the radio dial to off.

But it didn't cut off the girl's laughter.

The car was rolling past trees and houses again, following the curving road uphill. I barely noticed. I was trembling. I could still hear the roar and clatter of the speeding train cars in my mind.

"Who are you?" I finally choked out. "Are you a ghost? Do you haunt this car?"

No answer.

"I don't understand!" I cried. "Tell me who you are. Why did you try to kill me?"

Silence.

And then the soft moan, *"I'm evil ... I'm so evil."*

The car slowed to a stop.

I peered out the windshield — and to my surprise saw my parents, their robes flapping over their pajamas, running barefoot down the driveway.

I'm . . . home! I breathed a long, shuddering sigh of relief.

Dad pulled open the driver's door. "Mitchell!" he bellowed. "How could you *do* this?"

"How? How?" He grabbed my arm and tugged me out of the car. His eyes burned angrily into mine. I'd never seen him so angry.

Behind him, Mom shook her head. I saw tears on her cheeks.

"This is the worst thing you ever did," she choked out. "The worst."

"We can't believe you took the car," Dad said through gritted teeth. His hand squeezed my arm.

"But — but — I didn't do it!" I sputtered.

Dad's eyes gazed over my shoulder to the open car door. "Mitchell, you're in serious, serious trouble," he said, his voice trembling with anger. "Don't tell lies. Don't make up any stories. There's no one else in the car. Don't you dare try to tell us you didn't take it."

"But — I can explain!" I started.

I took a deep breath. Where should I start? How could I convince them that I didn't drive the car?

"Hey — what's going on?" A girl's voice cried out before I could start to explain.

I turned and saw Marissa jogging across the driveway.

"Is everything okay?" she called, her blond hair bobbing on her shoulders as she ran. "Why is everyone up so late?"

"Wh-who are *you*?" Mom blurted out, wiping tears off her cheeks. "Are you a friend of Mitchell's?"

"She just moved in," I told Mom.

"I'm Marissa Meddin," Marissa announced. "I was up late. I heard voices. I saw Mitchell out here. . . ." Her voice trailed off.

"Mitchell is in very big trouble," Dad said, finally releasing his grip on my arm. "Mitchell has done something really terrible."

Marissa's eyes locked on mine.

"It isn't true!" I cried. "Mom — Dad — you've got to believe me! I came out and sat in the car. But I didn't drive it away."

"Mitchell, that's ridiculous," Mom insisted.

"I'm warning you for the last time to tell the truth," Dad uttered angrily.

I couldn't hold it in any longer. "The car is haunted!" I screamed.

Mom and Dad cried out in surprise. Marissa stared at me openmouthed.

"I know you won't believe me — but it's true! I heard a girl's voice. She kept laughing and saying how evil she was. She drove the car. I didn't drive it. I couldn't control it. There's a ghost. Really. A ghost —"

"Mitchell, stop right now," Dad said. "Have you suddenly turned into Todd? We're not going to believe any crazy story about a ghost."

"You're just getting yourself into more trouble," Mom sighed.

"But she tried to *kill* me!" I wailed.

Marissa narrowed her eyes at me. Her expression changed. I saw her chin tremble. She suddenly looked very frightened. "Maybe Mitchell is telling the truth," she said softly.

I don't think Mom and Dad heard her.

"What was in your mind?" Mom demanded, more tears rolling down her cheeks. She pulled her bathrobe around her. "What were you thinking? Did you really think your dad and I wouldn't see that the car was missing?"

"You didn't think at all — did you, Mitchell?" Dad accused. "You wanted to drive the car so bad — so you just stole the keys and took it for a spin."

"But you're only twelve!" Mom cried.

"The car is haunted. I can prove it!" I insisted. "I'm telling the truth. I'll prove it to you."

I didn't give them a chance to stop me.

I turned and dove back to the car. "Come and listen," I ordered them. "There's a voice. The ghost's voice. It comes out of the speakers. She'll tell you. She'll tell you the truth."

I leaned into the car. They huddled close behind me.

I reached in and clicked on the radio.

"Go ahead," I told the voice. "Tell them what you did. Tell them the truth. Tell them why you haunt this car. *Tell* them!"

The next night after dinner, I was upstairs in my room talking to Steve on the phone. "I can only stay on for thirty seconds," I told him. "It's the new rule. I'm prisoner here in my own house."

"What's *that* about?" Steve asked.

"It'll take too long to explain," I sighed.

"So you're in trouble?" he asked.

"I'm grounded for life."

"Whoa! That's totally disturbing!" Steve exclaimed. "Why? What did you do?"

"My parents think I stole the new car and then lied about it," I told him.

"Did you do it?" he demanded. "Did you really take the car out?"

"Kind of," I replied.

Then my kitchen timer rang. My thirty seconds were up. "Have a nice life," I told Steve glumly. Then I hung up.

I slammed the timer onto my desk. Mom had

given it to me to time my phone calls. What can you say to someone in thirty seconds?

It wasn't fair.

The whole thing wasn't fair. I didn't do anything wrong.

But no one would ever believe me about the car being haunted.

Well . . . I suddenly remembered there was one person who would definitely believe me.

I made my way down the hall to Todd's room.

I heard him laughing in there. As I entered, I saw him leaning over his computer keyboard, staring into the monitor, playing a game.

He turned away from the screen when he heard me enter. "What's up?" he asked brightly. "Want to play me?"

"I can't," I moaned. "I'm not allowed to have any fun, remember?"

He frowned. "I never saw Mom and Dad so angry."

I slumped down on the edge of Todd's bed. "Do you believe me?" I asked him. "Do you believe my story about the ghost in the car?"

Todd nodded solemnly. "Yes. Of course I believe you," he replied, his voice just above a whisper. "And I know who the ghost is."

"Huh?" I gasped. "You do? You know?"

He nodded again.

I lurched across the room and grabbed him by the shoulders. "Todd — tell me," I demanded. "Who is it? Who is the ghost?"

"It's that new girl, Marissa," Todd said solemnly.

I gaped at him. "Excuse me?"

"It's Marissa," he repeated. "She's the one who is haunting the car."

I laughed. "That's totally crazy." I rolled my eyes. "Why did I even ask you? I should have known you'd come up with something totally insane."

"It isn't crazy," Todd replied softly. He sat down at the other end of the bed and crossed his arms over his chest. "She showed up here the same day as the car, right? And she always appears suddenly to let you out when the door sticks. Right?"

I scratched my head. "Yes. Right. But that doesn't prove anything."

"How come she is always there, even in the middle of the night?" Todd demanded. "Because she is a ghost. Because she haunts the car. I know it."

"That's totally dumb," I told him. "Marissa is a real girl, not a ghost. She doesn't live in the car. She moved onto our street last week. I'll prove it to you."

I jumped up, ran down the hall, and grabbed my cordless phone. Then I brought it back into Todd's room.

I punched in 411. "Hello? Information? I'd like the phone number of the Meddin family. They just moved in on Scotts Landing Road."

His arms still tightly crossed, Todd kept his eyes on me as I waited for the operator to find the number. I could see he was tense. He chewed his bottom lip.

"I'm sorry," the operator reported. "There is no listing for Meddin on Scotts Landing."

"Oh," I murmured. A chill ran down my back. I thanked her and clicked off the phone.

Then I turned to Todd. "Maybe they don't have their phone hooked up yet," I said. I grabbed his arm and tugged him to his feet. "Come on. Let's go."

"Huh? Go?" He pulled his arm free. "Go where?"

"Let's go over to Marissa's house," I replied. "I want to prove to you that she isn't a ghost."

"But — but you're grounded!" he sputtered. "You're not allowed to leave the house, Mitchell."

"Mom and Dad are in the basement," I told him. "Mom is helping Dad with some project he messed up. They'll be down there for hours. We'll be back before they notice we're gone."

We sneaked downstairs and grabbed flashlights and our jackets. I could hear Mom and Dad down in the basement, arguing. They always yell at each other when they work together on one of Dad's projects.

Todd and I crept out the front door. It was a cold, cloudy night. No moon or stars in the sky.

We jogged past the car. It sat dark and empty in the driveway. No green glow. No ghost grinning out at us from the front seat.

We made our way to the street. Nearby, something scampered over the carpet of dead leaves on the ground. Probably a squirrel.

"Which house did she move into?" Todd asked breathlessly.

I pointed to the next block. "The Faulkners' house," I said. "You know. The run-down brick house with the big front porch falling down."

The streetlight was out on the corner. Our flashlight beams danced over the dark pavement in front of us. It was a still, windless night. Nothing moved, nothing stirred.

The Faulkners' house was the second on the block. I could see from the corner that all the lights were out. No car in the driveway.

"Maybe they go to bed early," I murmured.

Our sneakers crunched over the dry brown

leaves that covered the front yard. Keeping our flashlights on the ground, we made our way up to the front porch.

The porch door was open, hanging off its hinges. I could see a pile of newspapers inside. And several crushed soda cans.

"See?" Todd whispered. "I told you. No one lives here."

"You're wrong," I insisted. I moved to the front window. I grabbed the window ledge and raised myself up on tiptoe.

Dark in the living room. Silent.

I shone the flashlight through the dust-smeared window.

"Whoa!" I murmured.

No furniture. An overturned paint bucket on the floor. Another pile of newspapers against one wall.

"What do you see?" Todd demanded.

"Nothing," I said. I moved around to the side of the house. I raised the flashlight to a side window. A bedroom. Empty. No furniture. No sign of life.

I lowered the light and turned to Todd. "No one lives here," I told him, shaking my head. "Marissa lied."

"She lives in the car," Todd insisted. "She haunts the car."

I stared hard at him. Was he right? Was Marissa a ghost?

How could I prove it to Mom and Dad?

I turned and stared at the dark, empty house. A chill rolled down my spine.

How could I prove to Mom and Dad that I was telling the truth?

Suddenly, I had an idea.

20

After school the next day, I had to stay late and help Steve and Allan with an art project. By the time I left the building, the sun was already setting. A pale half-moon rose over the bare trees.

Because of my punishment, I had orders to hurry straight home. But I had a mystery to solve — the mystery of the ghost in the car. And I knew there was only one person who could solve it.

Mr. Douglas, the man who sold us the car.

As I rode the bus to his neighborhood, I pictured Mr. Douglas's birdlike face, the long, crooked beak of a nose, the tiny, cold blue eyes.

Am I really doing this? I asked myself, peering out into the gray afternoon at the houses and trees whirring by. *Am I really going back to this man's house by myself to ask him if he sold us a haunted car?*

I swallowed hard and wiped my clammy hands on the legs of my jeans.

I knew I had no choice. I needed to know the truth. I needed to prove to my parents that I wasn't a liar.

I was so lost in my frightening thoughts, I missed the stop. I had to walk back four blocks. By the time I stepped onto Mr. Douglas's front stoop, my legs were shaking and my mouth was as dry as sand.

I could hear a TV on inside the house. I rang the bell.

Heavy footsteps. The door opened. Mr. Douglas peered out through the storm door, tilting his head suspiciously at me.

He was dressed the same as before, in a flannel shirt and denim overalls. His stringy hair was unbrushed, falling in tangles around his face.

"Uh . . . hi," I choked out. "Remember me?"

He just kept staring at me with those tiny bird-eyes.

I tried again. "My dad bought the car from you last week? Remember? Mr. Moinian?"

He nodded. He pushed open the storm door a few inches. "What can I do for you, young man?"

He raised his eyes to the street. I guessed he was searching for my dad. "How did you get here?"

"Took the bus," I told him. "I need to ask you some questions about the car, Mr. Douglas."

His eyes flashed. His mouth turned down in a scowl. "Sorry. I really don't have time right now." He started to pull the storm door closed.

"It won't take long," I insisted. "Some strange things have been happening. I was just wondering —"

"Sorry," he repeated. He suddenly looked very tense. "I really can't talk about the car now."

"Please," I pleaded. "Can I just come in for a second? I —"

"No. You can't come in. I have to ask you to leave now," he said sternly. He opened his mouth to say more — but his phone rang.

"Good-bye." He turned away and hurried to answer it.

"I don't get it," I muttered. "What is his problem?"

Why wouldn't he answer a few simple questions?

I stepped up to the top of the stoop, cupped my hands around my face, and peered into the living room through the glass storm door.

"Huh?" My eyes stopped at the mantel, and I gasped. I struggled to focus on what I saw there.

A large, framed photograph of a girl.

A lighted candle on each side of the photo. And

on a black ribbon under the photo, the words IN
LOVING MEMORY.

"No," I murmured. "No, it can't be."

Because I recognized the girl in the photograph.

The dead girl.

Marissa.

"You were right," I told Todd breathlessly as soon as I ran into the house.

He stared at me. "What do you mean?"

"Marissa is a ghost. She's dead. I saw her picture at Mr. Douglas's house. There were candles next to it, and a sign that said 'In Loving Memory.'"

Todd let out a long gasp. All the color drained from his face.

I felt bad. I realized I had scared him. *I shouldn't be telling Todd all this,* I decided. *He's too afraid of ghosts.*

"Wh-what are you going to do?" he stammered.

"Tell Mom and Dad," I replied. "I've got to warn them about Marissa. She's dangerous. The car is dangerous. Dad has to take it back to Mr. Douglas, before . . . before . . ."

"Before what?" Todd asked in a tiny voice.

I didn't answer. I didn't want to frighten him even more.

*   *   *

"The car is haunted. I can prove it," I announced as soon as the four of us sat down to dinner. "You know that girl Marissa who was here the other night?"

"Mitchell, can't we enjoy our dinner?" Dad interrupted angrily.

"You wanted pizza tonight, so we're having pizza," Mom chimed in. "So don't start an argument and spoil everyone's dinner."

"Spoil your dinner?" I shrieked.

I couldn't help it. I couldn't control myself.

I had this horrifying, unbelievable thing to tell them — and they were worried about me spoiling dinner?

I jumped to my feet. My chair fell behind me and clattered to the floor.

"Mitchell — sit down!" Dad ordered.

"The new car is haunted!" I screamed at the top of my lungs. *"There is a ghost in the car — and she's EVIL!"*

"He's telling the truth," Todd said softly. "It's really true."

"You keep out of it!" Dad warned him. "You're the one who started all this ghost nonsense around here, Todd."

"It *isn't* nonsense!" I wailed, shaking my fists above my head.

"Mitchell, take your plate," Mom ordered,

waving both hands. "Good-bye. Take your plate to your room and eat your pizza upstairs."

"But, Mom —"

"Go! Go! Go!" Dad ordered.

"But I'm telling the truth!" I cried.

"Not another word," Dad shouted, "or you'll be grounded for a *second* lifetime!"

Grumbling under my breath, I ran out of the dining room. I didn't take my plate. I didn't feel like eating.

I felt like screaming and crying and shoving my fist through a wall. Or jumping in the car and letting it take me anywhere it wanted.

Is there anything more horrible than knowing the truth about something important — and having your own parents refuse to believe you?

"I'm not a liar!" I screeched from the stairs. Then I ran up to my room, my heart pounding, my throat aching from all my screaming.

My phone was ringing when I burst into my room. I grabbed it. "Hello?" I demanded breathlessly.

"Mitchell? It's Marissa."

I gasped. "Huh? Marissa?"

"Listen, Mitchell, I called to warn you —"

I didn't wait for her to finish. "Marissa — I know the truth!" I blurted out.

Silence on her end. Then, finally, she murmured, "You do?"

94

"Yes," I replied in a trembling voice. "I know who you are. I know the truth about you."

Marissa's voice lowered to a cold whisper. "So what are you going to do, Mitchell?" she demanded. "Now that you know the truth, what are you going to do about it?"

Her whispered voice sent chills down my back.

I'm talking to a ghost, I realized. *And . . . she just threatened me.*

Trembling, I clicked off the phone and tossed it onto my bed. I took a deep breath and held it.

Calm . . . calm . . . I ordered myself. I shut my eyes and waited for my heart to stop racing.

I shoved my hands into my jeans pockets and began pacing back and forth. *What am I going to do now?* I asked myself. *What can I do?*

Is Marissa going to come after me? I wondered. *Now that I know the truth about her, is she going to try to stop me from telling her secret?*

Is she going to make me a ghost, too?

I sat down at my worktable and started to arrange the pieces of my car model. *Maybe working on the model will relax me,* I thought. *Maybe it will take my mind off Marissa.*

But after a few minutes, I was still sitting there, staring at the model pieces, my mind whirring.

When I heard Dad calling me from downstairs, I jumped up with a start.

I made my way to the stairs. I saw Mom, Dad, and Todd with their coats on. "Where are you going?" I asked, hurrying down the stairs.

"To Cousin Ella's — remember?" Mom replied, peering into the hall mirror, adjusting her scarf. "She's been sick all week. We promised to visit."

"And I'm coming, too?" I asked. I started for the coat closet.

"No. Why don't you stay home?" Mom suggested. "You need a cooling-off period."

"Some time by yourself, Mitchell," Dad chimed in. "Some time to think about how crazy you've been acting."

"But —" I started to protest. Then I sighed and shrugged. "Okay, fine. I'll stay home. I don't care."

Dad strode down the hall and clicked the lamp by the den. "The wire is still crackling," he murmured, shaking his head. "I can't find the short. Better be careful with this lamp, Mitchell."

"Do I have to kiss Ella?" Todd asked Mom. "Her makeup tastes terrible and it sticks to my lips."

"You don't have to kiss her," Mom told him. "She's sick, remember?"

I saw the car keys on the hallway table. "Are you taking the car?" I asked Dad.

"You know that Martin is picking us up," Dad replied. "We told you a hundred times."

"But you'd better stay away from that car," Mom warned. She narrowed her eyes sharply at me. "I mean it, Mitchell. Don't go near it. Don't sit in it. Don't touch it."

"Don't worry," I muttered.

They don't have to worry. No way *I'm climbing into a haunted car!* I told myself.

I followed them outside. We stood on the driveway until my cousin Martin pulled up in his green Taurus.

"Tell Ella I hope she feels better," I said. I waved to my cousin.

Todd and Dad climbed into the back. Mom started to climb into the front passenger seat, then turned back to me. "Mitchell, you'll be okay by yourself?"

"Yeah. Sure. No problem," I told her. "I stay by myself a lot, don't I?"

"Well, we'll be back early," she said. She closed the door after her.

I watched the green Taurus back away and head down the road toward town.

I was standing next to our new car. The driver's window was down a couple of inches. I lowered my face to it.

"Marissa — are you in there?" I called.

No reply.

Light from the streetlamp made the creamy interior glow.

"Marissa — can you hear me?" I called in.

Still no answer.

But I felt a strong tug. As if someone was pulling me, pulling me into the car.

"No!" I uttered out loud. "No. I'm not climbing in."

I wanted to walk away. I wanted desperately to get to the safety of my house.

But an invisible force was pulling me . . . pulling me.

"No . . . please — let me go!" I pleaded.

Pulling . . . pulling . . .

I gripped the door handle.

And started to open the door.

No, Mitchell. Get away! I warned myself.

Don't do this.

Don't get into this car!

I pulled open the door. The seats and dashboard glowed brighter . . . brighter. I blinked in the pulsing white light.

Get away, Mitchell. Get away while you have a chance.

I slid behind the wheel, slid into the pulsing, bright light.

I closed the car door.

My hands wrapped around the steering wheel, so cool, so smooth.

I heard the door locks click down. I knew I was locked in once again.

I blinked hard, waiting for my eyes to adjust to the throbbing brightness.

It took me a long time to realize that I wasn't alone.

I turned and saw someone beside me in the passenger seat.

A blond-haired girl dressed all in black.

I couldn't see her face. She had her back turned to me. But I knew who it was.

"Marissa!" I choked out.

She turned slowly — and I opened my mouth in a scream of horror.

Not Marissa!

I was staring at a hideous ghoul. Purple, rotted skin, lined and rutted like a decayed prune. Inky black eyes sunk back in deep sockets. Pulsing red veins up and down a broken nose. Toothless green gums, swollen and dripping with yellow slime. Torn lips twisted in an ugly grin.

"Ohhhh," I moaned as the foul smell of the creature floated into my nostrils.

I tried to turn away as she brought her face close to mine. So close I could see two long white worms wriggling in her nose.

Her blond hair brushed my face, stiff as straw, crawling with bugs.

Her hot, sour breath swept over me, sickening me, making my stomach heave. Her swollen green gums clicked together as she whispered, *"I'm evil . . . I'm so evil."*

My stomach heaved again. I swallowed hard, struggling to keep from vomiting.

Her hair brushed against my cheek again, scratching my skin, making my face tingle and itch.

I shivered in the sudden cold. So cold inside the car, so cold the windows steamed.

Cold as death, I thought.

Her whispered words sent another cloud of foul breath over me: *"I'm so evil, Mitchell. So evil."*

"Noooooooo!" I screamed again.

I twisted away from her rotting, toothless face.

I pulled the door handle. I shoved all my weight against the door.

I clawed at the windows. I pounded my fists against the glass.

"Help me! Somebody — help me! Let me out of here!" My voice high and shrill, trembling in the frozen, sour air.

"Please — let me out!"

I turned to see her toss back her head. She opened her mouth in an ugly laugh. It sounded more like dry heaves than laughing.

"*So evil . . .*"

And then, as I gaped in frozen horror, her wet black eyes rolled back in their sockets. Her rutted purple skin began to sag. To melt.

She slumped forward. Her head thumped the dashboard. Her stiff blond hair wriggled like worms.

Her whole body shook as she melted. Melted away, smaller . . . smaller.

I didn't move. I didn't breathe.

Hugging myself in the frigid cold, I watched her melt away. Until her body vanished, and a cloud of glowing green gas floated over the passenger seat.

And then the gas faded, darkened, vanished.

My chest ached. I realized I hadn't taken a breath. I let my air out in a long *WHOOSH*.

"Hello?" I called in a weak voice. "Are you still here?"

The car started up, as if in reply.

The engine roared. The gearshift moved into reverse.

"No — wait!" I gasped.

The car jolted down the driveway, onto the street. It shifted into drive — and shot forward. The tires squealed as it swerved wildly to one side of the road, then the other.

I grabbed the wheel, frantically tried to turn around. But the car wasn't in my control.

"No!" I cried out as the car jumped off the road. Bumped along the grass. Swiped a tall hedge. Bounced back onto the road, spinning wildly.

"Stop it! Stop the car!" I screamed. "Who are you? Why are you doing this?"

Over the squeal of the tires, the roar of the engine, I heard the girl's laughter.

"Why?" I screamed. "Why? Tell me! I have to know!"

The car hurtled down the middle of the road, squealing out of control, tilting crazily around the turns, faster, faster.

And the girl's voice floated out of the speakers: *"I died in this car, Mitchell. And now it's your turn!"*

"No — wait!" I pleaded. "Listen to me. I — I don't want to die!"

Once again, I heard her laughter.

The car swerved off the road, scraped against a tree, bounced back onto the pavement.

I'm going to die, I realized.

She's going to crash the car. And I'm totally helpless. I can't do anything to save myself.

The car skidded and spun around twice. Then it continued hurtling down the curving road toward town and the valley.

"Please —" I started. But the words choked in my throat. "I — I don't understand."

"I was only fourteen." Her voice rose so lifelessly from the speakers. *"Only fourteen, Mitchell."*

"I'm only twelve!" I cried. My head crashed hard against the window as the car veered sharply off the road again.

And then I heard the sirens. Rising and falling. Close behind me.

A police car!

They'll save me! I realized. *They'll stop the car. They'll get me out!*

With a happy cry, I slammed my foot down hard on the brake.

The pedal slid to the floor. But the car roared forward.

Behind me, the siren wailed, closer.

"Slow down!" I screamed. "It's the police. Slow the car down!"

Her hard, cruel laughter rang out over the shrill siren.

I jammed the brake down again. Again.

I could see the flashing red lights in the mirror now.

Can the police catch up? I wondered. *Can they stop this car? Can they rescue me before I crash?*

The shrill siren wailed so close behind me.

The red lights flashed brightly in the mirror.

And then passed by on the left. Passed my speeding car.

And I saw that it wasn't a police car. It was a long red fire truck.

It swerved past me, siren blaring, and kept going.

I stared at the back of the fire truck, twin ladders poking from the sides. And then it vanished around a curve.

I let out a long, disappointed sigh.

"Only fourteen," the girl's voice repeated, as if the fire truck hadn't even existed.

The car hurtled down the middle of the road, spinning so close to the edge of the hill.

"Only fourteen. I took the car out for a drive. I crashed it, Mitchell. I died. I've haunted the car ever since, waiting . . . waiting for someone to join me, to keep me company. And now I've found you."

"No — please!" I screamed.

The car bounced hard. My head slammed into the ceiling.

"I'm sorry you died," I told her. "I'm really sorry. But I don't want to join you. Please — take me home!"

Silence.

And then the car went into a skid. The tires squealed over the pavement.

The car spun wildly. Once. Twice.

Spun completely around.

"You want to go home?" the ghost asked.

"Yes!" I cried. "Yes! Take me home!"

"Okay," she replied, her voice as cold as the air in the car. *"Okay, Mitchell. I'll take you home."*

The car jolted forward. Gripping the bouncing wheel, I peered out through the windshield and realized we were headed back up the hill.

Toward my house.

"You're doing it?" I cried, my heart racing. "You're taking me home?"

"If that's where you want to die," she replied. *"You can die just as easily against the front of your house."*

"No, wait —"

The car picked up speed. It felt as if we were flying now, flying around the curves, following the road as it twisted uphill.

Houses shot past in a gray blur. I recognized the neighborhood. And then I recognized my block.

Faster. Faster.

I pumped the brakes. I spun the wheel.

Helpless. I was totally helpless.

She's going to smash the car into the front of my house, I knew.

"*It won't hurt for long*," the ghost murmured as if reading my thoughts. "*And then we'll be together forever.*"

I shut my eyes.

The car squealed to a stop. I heard the screech of skidding tires.

I opened my eyes — and saw a wall of orange. Flames!

My house! My house was on fire!

Fire trucks were scattered over the front yard. Solemn-faced neighbors huddled in the driveway.

Was that Todd? Yes. Todd standing with my parents, their faces caught in the flickering, orange light, their expressions so worried, so horrified.

"I — I would have been inside the house," I stammered to the ghost. "I would have been asleep in there. I would have died. But you saved me. You saved my life!"

"*Noooooooooo!*" I heard her howl in horror.

And then I saw her again. The hideous, ghoulish face. The blond hair, stiff as straw. The dead girl, dead and decayed, all in black.

She sat beside me again, her toothless mouth open in a scream of horror. She raised bony hands and tore at her hair, tore off hunks of it, revealing cracked gray skull bone underneath.

"Noooooo!" she wailed. *"I'm evil! I'm so evil! My mission is evil!"*

"But — you saved my life!" I protested.

"I've failed! Failed!" she shrieked, ripping out hunk after hunk of her hair.

Her inky black eyes turned to me, glowing with hatred. *"I have failed. I have accidentally done GOOD! And now I must pay. Now I must die forever!"*

Once again, she started to shrink, to melt away.

The wet eyes rolled from their sockets. Plopped onto her lap. Her skull cracked open. Her body slumped forward.

I stared helplessly as she melted away. Shrank and melted until nothing was left but a puddle of thick green slime on the car seat. And then the slime melted away, too.

The car door swung open.

Strong hands pulled me out.

Dad wrapped me in a hug. Then Mom joined in.

"You're okay! Mitchell — you're okay!" Mom kept repeating, holding me close.

"We — we thought you were trapped inside!" Dad declared.

Todd had tears running down his cheeks. He

rushed across the grass to hug me, too. "I thought you were on fire," he murmured.

"The ghost saved me," I told them, shouting over the roar of the flames and the rush of the fire hoses. "The ghost drove me away in the car. She saved my life."

Mom and Dad exchanged glances. I could see that they didn't believe me.

But I didn't care. I was so glad to be back safe.

All four of us jumped as part of our roof fell with a crash into the leaping flames.

"It's all my fault," Dad sighed, shaking his head. "I should never have tried to fix the wiring. From now on, I'm never going to fool around with electricity again."

"It's okay," Mom said, her arms around Todd and me. "We're all safe. All of us."

"I was right," Todd whispered to me. "The car was haunted. And it was Marissa, right?"

"Yes," I replied uncertainly. "You were right, Todd. You knew. You —"

I stopped when I saw her standing near the car.

The ghost.

Marissa.

"Mitchell!" Marissa cried, running over to me, her blond hair flying behind her.

I took a step back. My throat tightened. "You — you told me in the car that now you would die forever," I gasped.

"Huh?" She narrowed her eyes at me. "Mitchell — you're okay?"

"Don't pretend. Don't act innocent," I replied sharply. "You're not fooling anyone. You're evil!"

Her expression changed. She grabbed my arm roughly. "Come over here, Mitchell."

"No!" I protested. "Haven't you done enough? Please —"

I tried to pull away. But she dragged me toward the street.

"Why are you doing this?" I cried. "I know you're the ghost, Marissa. I went to your father's house. I saw your portrait and the candles on the mantel."

She tightened her grip on my arm. Her eyes

burned into mine. "I'm alive, Mitchell," she whispered, bringing her face close to mine. "See? I'm real." She squeezed my arm.

"But —" I started.

"That photo you saw," Marissa continued, not letting go. "That was my twin sister, Becka. Becka was so evil."

"Your sister?" I choked out.

"Last summer, Becka took the car. She didn't know how to drive. She crashed and killed herself." Marissa's voice cracked with emotion. "It broke my father's heart. He's never been the same." She lowered her eyes.

"I'm . . . sorry," I muttered.

"Dad was desperate to sell the car," Marissa continued after taking a deep breath. "He didn't want the car Becka died in. When I saw your father buy it, I decided I had to warn you."

"Warn me?" I cried. I pulled my arm free from her grip. "You mean you *knew* your sister was haunting the car? You *knew* she planned to kill me?"

Marissa nodded.

"How?" I demanded. "How did you know?"

"She told me," Marissa replied. "I was sitting in the car one day, waiting for my dad. Becka appeared. All ugly and dead. She told me she haunted the car now. She told me she'd haunt the car until she got revenge — revenge for dying so young."

"So why didn't you tell me?" I asked. "Why didn't you —"

"I wanted to," Marissa interrupted. "But I didn't think you'd believe me. So I waited. And then on the phone, you told me you *knew* the truth — remember? So I figured if you knew, I didn't have to warn you."

"Becka saved my life," I told Marissa. "She didn't mean to. But she did."

A strange smile spread over Marissa's face. She wiped tears from her eyes. Then she turned to the car.

"Poor Mitchell." She sighed. "You were so excited about the new car. . . ."

"Uh . . . that's okay," I replied with a shudder. "I've kind of lost my interest in cars. I think maybe I'll get into baseball or hockey or something."

We spent the night at the O'Connors' house, next door. The following morning, Mom fretted over me at breakfast. "Your dad and I are very worried about you, Mitchell. All this talk about ghosts."

"But, Mom —" I started.

"You're frightening Todd with all your ghost stories," she continued. "And he was already frightened before you began."

I sighed and shoved my cereal bowl away. "Mom — what do you want me to do? I've been trying to tell you the truth. But you and Dad refuse —"

"Enough," she insisted sharply. "I want you to

115

talk to Todd. Tell him you made up the ghost story. Tell him the car isn't haunted."

"But, Mom —" I tried again.

This time, Dad interrupted. He came lumbering through the back door from outside, shaking his head. "I've got to drive to town," he grumbled, "but the car won't start. I called the guy from the garage and —"

A knock on the door.

We all turned to see a man in a gray work uniform, carrying a big toolbox. "You called the garage?" he asked.

"Yeah. The blue car out front. It won't start," Dad said. "Here, I'll show you."

I followed them out to the car. Next door, the ruins of our house still smoldered. The yard was littered with broken glass and hunks of blackened wood. The air smelled smoky and sour.

The guy from the garage pulled up the hood of the car. He leaned in over the engine. Then he quickly stood back up and squinted at Dad. "This is a joke, right?"

Dad gaped at him. "Joke?"

The man pointed to the engine. "I think the car would probably start *if you had a battery*!"

Dad stepped up beside him and peered under the hood. "Hey — you're right. I don't believe it. There's no battery."

Dad turned and stared at me. "No battery," he murmured, his face twisted in confusion. "No battery. But we've been driving it anyway. And it ran last night . . ."

I couldn't keep a grin from spreading over my face.

It's going to take Mom and Dad a while, I told myself. *But I think they're finally going to believe me!*

Want more chills?

Check out

Goosebumps®

THE BLOB THAT ATE EVERYONE

Here's a sneak peek!

"I used to believe in monsters," Alex said. She pushed her glasses up on her nose. Her nose twitched. With her pink face and round cheeks, she looked like a tall, blond bunny rabbit.

"When I was little, I thought that a monster lived in my sock drawer," Alex told me. "You won't believe this, Zackie. But I never opened that drawer. I used to wear my sneakers without socks. Sometimes I tried to go barefoot to kindergarten. I was too scared to open that drawer. I knew the sock monster would bite my hand off!"

She laughed. Alex has the strangest laugh. It sounds more like a whistle than a laugh. *"Wheeeeeeh! Wheeeeeh!"*

She shook her head, and her blond ponytail shook with her. "Now that I'm twelve, I'm a lot smarter," she said. "Now I know that there is no such thing as monsters."

That's what Alex said to me *two seconds* before we were attacked by the monster.

*   *   *

It was spring vacation, and Alex and I were out collecting things. That's what we do when we can't think of anything better.

Sometimes we collect weird-looking weeds. Sometimes we collect bugs. Or odd-shaped leaves.

Once, we collected stones that looked like famous people. That didn't last long. We couldn't find too many.

If you get the idea that Norwood Village is a boring town — you're right!

I mean, it *was* boring until the monster attacked.

Alex Iarocci lives next door to me. And she is my best friend.

Adam Levin, who lives across town, is my best friend, too. I think a person should have a *lot* of best friends!

I'm not sure why Alex has a boy's name. I think it's short for Alexandria. But she won't tell me.

She complains about her name all the time. It gives her a lot of trouble.

Last year at school, Alex was assigned to a boys' gym class. And she gets mail addressed to *Mr.* Alex Iarocci.

Sometimes people have trouble with my name, too. Zackie Beauchamp. My last name is pronounced BEECH-am. But no one ever knows how to say it.

Why am I going on about names like this?

I think I know why.

You see, when the Blob Monster attacked, I was so scared, I forgot my own name!

Alex and I had decided to collect worms. Only purple worms — no brown ones.

That made the search more interesting.

It had rained the day before, a long, steady, spring rain. Our backyards were still soft and spongy.

The worms were coming up for air. They poked through the wet grass. And wriggled onto the driveway.

We were both crouched down, searching for purple ones — when I heard a loud, squishy sound behind me.

I spun around quickly.

And gasped when I saw the monster. "Alex — look!"

She turned, too. And a whistling sound escaped her mouth. "*Wheeeeh!*" Only *this* time, she wasn't laughing.

I dropped the worm I had been carrying and took a *biiig* step back.

"It — it looks like a giant human heart!" Alex cried.

She was right.

The monster made another loud *squish* as it bounced over the grass toward us. It bounced like a giant beach ball, taller than Alex and me. Nearly as tall as the garage!

It was pink and wet. And throbbing.

BRUM BRRUUM BRUMMM. It pulsed like a heart.

It had two tiny black eyes. The eyes glowed and stared straight ahead.

On top of the pink blob, I thought I saw curled-up snakes. But as I stared in horror, I realized they weren't snakes. They were thick, purple veins — arteries tied together in a knot.

BRRUUUM BRUM BRUMM.

The monster throbbed and bounced.

"Ohhhhhh!" I groaned as I saw the sticky trail of white slime it left behind on the grass.

Alex and I were taking giant steps — backward. We didn't want to turn our backs on the ugly thing.

"Unh unh unh!" Terrified groans escaped my throat. My heart had to be pounding at a hundred miles an hour!

I took another step back. Then another.

And as I backed away, I saw a crack open up in the creature's middle.

At first I thought the pink blob was cracking apart.

But as the crack grew wider, I realized I was staring at its mouth.

The mouth opened wider. Wider.

Wide enough to swallow a human!

And then a fat purple tongue plopped out. The tongue made a wet *SPLAT* as it hit the grass.

"Ohhhhh." I groaned again. My stomach lurched. I nearly lost my lunch.

The end of the tongue was shaped like a shovel. A fat, sticky, purple shovel.

To shovel people into the gaping mouth?

Thick, white slime poured from the monster's mouth. "It — it's *drooling!*" I choked out.

"Run!" Alex cried.

I turned — and tripped on the edge of the driveway.

I landed hard on my elbows and knees.

And looked back — in time to see the drooling, pink mouth open wider as the tongue wrapped around me . . . pulling me, pulling me in.

Alex stared at me, her mouth open wide. "Zackie, that is *awesome!*" she declared.

Adam scratched his curly black hair and made a face. "You call that scary?" He rolled his eyes. "That's about as scary as *Goldilocks and the Three Bears.*"

I held the pages of my story in one hand. I rolled them up and took a swing at Adam with them.

He laughed and ducked out of my reach.

"That is an awesome story!" Alex repeated. "What do you call it?"

"'Adventure of the Blob Monster,'" I told her.

"Oh, wow," Adam exclaimed sarcastically. "Did you think that up all by yourself?"

Alex gave Adam a hard shove that sent him tumbling onto the couch. "Give Zackie a break," she muttered.

The three of us were hanging out in Adam's house. We were squeezed into what his parents call the rec room.

The room is so small. Only a couch and a TV fit.

It was spring vacation, and we were hanging out because we didn't know what else to do. The night before, I stayed up till midnight, working on my scary story about the Blob Monster.

I want to be a writer when I grow up. I write scary stories all the time. Then I read them to Alex and Adam.

They always react in the same way. Alex always likes my stories. She thinks they're really scary. She says that my stories are so good, they give her nightmares.

Adam always says my stories aren't scary at all. He says he can write better stories with one hand tied behind his back.

But he never does.

Adam is big and red-cheeked and chubby. He looks a little like a bear. He likes to punch people and wrestle around. Just for fun. He's actually a good guy.

He just never likes my stories.

"What's wrong with this story?" I asked him.

The three of us were crammed onto the couch now. There was nowhere else to sit.

"Stories never scare me," Adam replied. He picked an ant off the couch arm, put it between his thumb and finger, and shot it at me.

He missed.

"I thought the story was *really* scary," Alex said. "I thought you had really good description."

"I *never* get scared by books or stories," Adam insisted. "Especially stories about dumb monsters."

"Well — what *does* scare you?" Alex demanded.

"Nothing," Adam bragged. "I don't get scared by movies, either. Nothing ever scares me."

And then he opened his mouth wide in a scream of horror.

All three of us did.

We leaped off the couch — as a terrifying *screech* rang through the room.

And a black shadow swept over the floor.

About the Author

R.L. Stine's books are read all over the world. So far, his books have sold more than 300 million copies, making him one of the most popular children's authors in history. Besides Goosebumps, R.L. Stine has written the teen series Fear Street and the funny series Rotten School, as well as the Mostly Ghostly series, The Nightmare Room series, and the two-book thriller *Dangerous Girls*. R.L. Stine lives in New York with his wife, Jane, and Minnie, his King Charles spaniel. You can learn more about him at www.RLStine.com.

NOW A MAJOR
MOTION PICTURE

JACK BLACK

Goosebumps

THERE'S ALWAYS ROOM FOR ONE MORE SCREAM!

An all-new series from fright-master R.L. Stine!

THE ORIGINAL Goosebumps BOOKS
WITH AN ALL-NEW LOOK!

R.L. Stine's
Life Story

REVENGE OF THE LIVING DUMMY
R.L. STINE

CREEP FROM THE DEEP
R.L. STINE

MONSTER BLOOD FOR BREAKFAST!
R.L. STINE

THE SCREAM OF THE HAUNTED MASK
R.L. STINE

DR. MANIAC VS. ROBBY SCHWARTZ
R.L. STINE

WHO'S YOUR MUMMY?
R.L. STINE

MY FRIENDS CALL ME MONSTER
R.L. STINE

SAY CHEESE - AND DIE SCREAMING!
R.L. STINE

WELCOME TO CAMP SLITHER
R.L. STINE

THE SCARIEST PLACE ON EARTH!

Catch the MOST WANTED Goosebumps® villains UNDEAD OR ALIVE!